Macmillan
Children's Guide to Endangered Animals

Giant panda

Previous page: Resplendent quetzal

Facing page: Hochstetter's frog

Macmillan
Children's Guide to Endangered Animals

ROGER FEW

Macmillian Publishing Company   New York

Maxwell Macmillan International
New York   Oxford   Singapore   Sydney

A Marshall Edition
This book was conceived, edited, and designed
by Marshall Editions,
170 Piccadilly, London W1V 9DD

Macmillan Publishing Company is part of the
Maxwell Communication Group of Companies.

Macmillan Publishing Company
866 Third Avenue
New York, NY 10022

First American edition
10 9 8 7 6 5 4 3 2 1

Film supplied by Dorchester Typesetting Group, UK
Origination by Chroma Graphics, Singapore
Printed and bound in Italy by New Interlitho SpA,
Milan

Library of Congress Cataloging-in-Publication Data

Few, Roger.
    Macmillan children's guide to endangered animals /
Roger Few. —1st American ed.
        p.   cm.
    "A Marshall edition" —T.p. verso.
    Includes index.
    Summary: Describes endangered species
throughout the world, the factors that threaten their
survival, and current efforts to save them from extinction.
    ISBN 0-02-734545-9
    1. Endangered species —Juvenile literature.
2. Wildlife conservation—Juvenile literature. [1. Rare
animals. 2. Wildlife conservation.] I. Title. II. Title:
Children's guide to endangered species.
QL83.F48 1993
591.52'9—dc20   92-41433

CONTENTS

Bridled nail-tail wallaby

FOREWORD

Earth, our home, is a strange and wonderful place. Its neighboring planets are utterly lifeless. But earth's atmosphere makes it an oasis in space. It is rich in habitats, from coral reefs to mountain peaks, that are living places for an incredible variety of plants and animals.

Dalmatian pelican

Scientists are amazed by the diversity of life on earth. More than 1.5 million kinds, or species, of living things have been named so far. Although most species of mammals, birds, and fishes are known, millions of species of insects and other small creatures await discovery. Some scientists believe that earth may be home to thirty million species of insects alone.

Whatever the total number of species, we know very little about most life on earth. We have learned a lot about certain animals and food plants, but little about all the other living organisms. Their lives are mysteries, as are their links with other living things, their roles in nature, and their possible value to humans.

It would be tragic to destroy so much of earth's life before it has been discovered and studied, but that is what people are doing. We are causing a rapid and massive loss of earth's great wealth of plants and animals, mostly by changing or wiping out wild habitats.

This detailed guide explains why extinctions are occurring, and what people can do to save species in danger. It explores forests, deserts, and other habitats in earth's seven geographical regions. For each region, a special "Focus" feature looks more closely at an endangered species and efforts to save it.

A variety of endangered animals from each habitat are described and illustrated in color. They include the well-known African elephant and whooping crane, but also salamanders, curlews, ghost bats, and many other less familiar creatures.

Most endangered species are not well known. Many are not cute or appealing to humans. Some, such as bats, are disliked and misunderstood by many people. Nevertheless, these creatures often play vital roles in nature. They are all part of the only life known to exist in the universe, and worth a great effort to keep alive in the wild habitats of this home we share.

Laurence Pringle

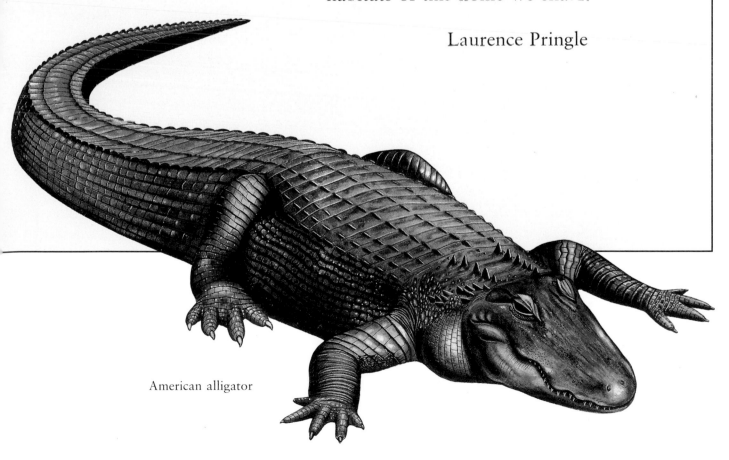

American alligator

Wildlife under threat

Animals of all kinds have been struggling to survive as our world changes. Day by day people require ever more space, more food, more water, more belongings, more fuel, and more roads. All these demands put a squeeze on the earth's resources, including its wildlife.

The biggest problem for wildlife today is that as people destroy and change natural landscapes, animals lose the places they need to live in, to find food and shelter. Wildlife habitats disappear to make way for farms, roads, cities, factories, and mines. Some animals are still able to survive in the changed landscapes. Farms, for example, can provide new types of food for wildlife. But they are unlikely to have lots of wild animals unless they still have plenty of trees, hedgerows, and other wild corners to provide shelter.

People do not even have to destroy habitats to make them unsuitable for animals. Sometimes a few changes simply make life too difficult. Dams on rivers, for instance, stop fish from moving up and downstream. Too many cattle or sheep put out to pasture in natural grasslands can thin out the foliage too much for wildlife because of grazing and trampling.

The loss of some habitats is particularly worrying. Wetlands — marshes, bogs, and swamps — are disappearing fast all over the world as people drain the water from them or fill them with earth. Afterward the soil is dry enough for farming or other uses, but many kinds of water creatures and birds will have lost their homes. Tropical forests are the only habitat for millions of animal species, but they, too, are shrinking year by year because the trees are being chopped down for wood and cleared away to make space for farms, ranches, and plantations. Even if the plots are later abandoned, plants grow poorly in the sun-baked soil. Centuries may pass before forests again cover the land.

Pollution is another serious threat to wildlife,

especially in areas where lots of people live. Carelessly thrown away garbage, sewage, and chemicals contaminate the soil, rivers, and the sea, and gases from factories and cars pollute the air. Too much pollution can ruin an animal's habitat and even kill it if it gets into its body. If farmers spray a strong chemical on their crops to kill pests, it can poison lots of other animals that live around farms because it gets into the food they eat.

Animals also die directly at the hands of people through hunting and fishing. Wild animals are killed for food, for sport, and for their skin, fur, horns, or shells. Too many hunters chasing one particular kind of animal may wipe it out entirely. Farmers also have guns and set traps to protect their crops and livestock from wild animals. Wolves, for

The terrible oil spills and fires started during the 1991 Gulf War destroyed countless animals. Many birds migrating across the area were also killed. Some were coated with soot from the thick smoke. Others died when they flew down to the oil lakes, mistaking the gleaming surface for water.

Oil pollution at sea is dangerous for wildlife because it forms a thick layer, or slick, on top of the water. Any bird that swims onto it gets its feathers so matted with oil that it cannot fly away. When it tries to clean its plumage with its bill it is likely to swallow so much oil that it dies.

instance, have long been persecuted wherever they occur because people fear that they attack farm animals. As a result, many species of wolves are now endangered.

Parrots and tortoises both make popular pets. But catching them and keeping them in captivity depletes their wild populations, especially if there are lots of pet shops overseas that want to buy them. Several species of parrots and tortoises, as well as other animals, have become endangered because of this. Wild apes are still captured for medical experiments although this trade is now illegal. One of the saddest things about the capture of wildlife is that many of the animals that are caught and taken away from their natural habitats die before they reach their destination.

Transporting animals around the world can itself be a threat to wildlife, especially if they are set free to roam wild in their new home. Releasing animals, on purpose or accidentally, in places where they did not live before is called introduction. People have taken cats, dogs, and farm animals with them around the world and some of them now roam free in the wild. Rabbits have been released in new areas to provide food, fur, and sport for hunters, and rats have spread around the world on their own by escaping from ships. An introduced animal can be dangerous because it may not have any natural enemies to keep its numbers down. It can easily upset the balance of nature by eating too much of another animal's food or being too good at hunting native wildlife.

Counting the costs

It is normal in nature for animals to rise and fall in number. Occasionally one kind may die out completely, becoming extinct. But changes like this usually happen very slowly over many generations. In today's world, however, the threats to wildlife are so great that thousands upon thousands of species are becoming scarce at the same time.

Some types of animals are especially vulnerable to threats. Large animals, such as rhinoceroses, need plenty of wild habitat to live in and their numbers are not very high in the first place. Because poachers can make a big profit by selling rhino horn they are ready to go far and wide to find the animals, and so all the rhinos in a large area can be killed off in a short time. Together, the five species of rhinoceros once ranged over most of Africa and tropical Asia, but they have entirely disappeared from all but a handful of places.

Other species are at risk because they never had much space. Their original home might be a single lake, an isolated patch of forest or a far-flung island. If people start to hunt one of these animals or ruin its habitat, it has nowhere else to hide and may quickly die out. Even if the threat is stopped it may be too late. The animal's population may already be so low that an outbreak of disease, a powerful storm, or any other natural disaster could easily finish it off.

Distant island animals are especially vulnerable for another reason. Because they are hard to reach, islands usually have far fewer species on them than the mainland. The animals that do live there may not have many natural enemies and are not adapted for defending themselves from attack. This makes them easy prey for human hunters and new animals such as rats and cats that people introduce to the islands. In fact, there are so many endangered animals on islands that they have a chapter at the end of the book all to themselves.

Keeping a record of which animals are endangered is one of the jobs of the IUCN, the

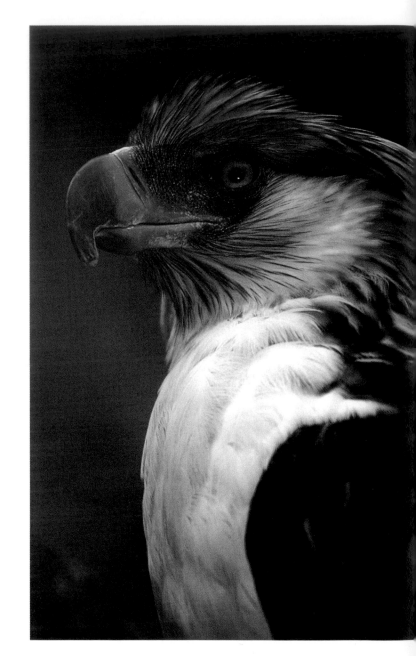

International Union for Conservation of Nature and Natural Resources. By collecting together lots of information on an animal species thought to be endangered, the IUCN can work out roughly how much its population has fallen in recent years, what sorts of threats it faces, and whether anything is being done to protect it. Then it can say how badly the animal is threatened and what more could be done to try to save it. The IUCN's Red Data Books are a good way of finding out which of the world's animals are in danger.

The Philippine eagle is one of the world's most endangered birds. There are probably fewer than 200 of these magnificent birds of prey left in the wild. A powerful predator big enough to catch monkeys, the eagle needs large areas of rain forest in which to hunt. But much of its home in the Philippines has already been destroyed and the rest is under threat from logging.

AT THE BRINK OF EXTINCTION

Here are some of the birds and mammals in this book that are likely to become extinct very soon:

Eskimo curlew

Kauai o-o

Ivory-billed woodpecker

Indigo macaw

Mountain gorilla

Madagascar fish eagle

Hermit ibis

Mediterranean monk seal

Baiji dolphin

Sumatran rhinoceros

White-eyed river martin

Kakapo

EXTINCT ANIMALS

Great auk

Dodo

Steller's sea cow

Quagga

Some animals have already been driven to extinction. Over the last 400 years, about one kind of mammal or bird has disappeared from the earth every year, including such fascinating creatures as the great auk and the dodo (both flightless birds), Steller's sea cow (a giant water mammal), and the quagga (a half-striped zebra). Many more animals all over the world are now endangered— their numbers have fallen so low that they, too, are likely to die out and follow these animals into extinction.

Saving species

Just as people are responsible for putting the future of so many animals at risk, so we have the power to make their future safer. It is very difficult to stop the things that threaten wildlife but lots of people now want to give endangered species a chance to survive. Actions to help wild animals are called wildlife conservation.

One of the simplest steps of wildlife conservation is to make laws that reduce or stop the killing and hunting of threatened animals. Most nations have such laws. When strictly enforced, they give threatened or endangered animals a chance to recover. Sometimes, international controls are needed, like the 1986 agreement to stop all whaling across the oceans.

CITES stands for the Convention on International Trade in Endangered Species of Wild Fauna and Flora. The 112 countries that belong to CITES meet regularly to decide controls for all kinds of threatened wildlife. Many species are listed in CITES' highest category, which means that no

country should allow animal traders to take them into or out of its ports. This includes live or stuffed specimens and any products from the animals such as meat, shells, skins, or horns.

But bans and controls do not always work. Many protected animals are still shot illegally by poachers, and it is sometimes quite easy to smuggle them abroad. Some people are prepared to break wildlife laws, especially if others will pay them lots of money for the animals or for animal products. One answer to this is to allow people to breed a threatened animal in captivity and sell the captive or farmed animals rather than take ones from the wild population. This has already helped some species of crocodiles and alligators, which are farmed in large numbers for their meat and hide.

Other ways of protecting individual species can cost a lot of time and money, and it is mainly in the richer countries that conservation groups have the means to do them. In New Zealand, where introduced animals threaten lots of native wildlife,

The efforts of campaigning groups such as Greenpeace have helped give the world's great whales a chance to recover after years of intensive whaling. In 1986 the International Whaling Commission agreed to stop all commercial hunting of whales after a lot of pressure from people and organizations all over the world. Several species, including the mighty blue whale, had been hunted so ruthlessly that they were fast heading toward extinction.

Even though there has been no commercial whaling since 1986 it will take many more years for the populations of great whales to build up. And, already, some countries want to start hunting the whales again.

conservationists have rounded up several highly endangered species and flown them to offshore islands that are free of rats and other threats.

If a species is in grave danger in the wild and is unlikely to survive, the only way to save it from extinction may be to capture some animals and keep them safe in captivity, often in zoos. Conservationists then need to encourage them to mate and raise young, which is not always easy because the animals may not breed in the unnatural conditions of captivity.

If captive-breeding is successful there may be enough animals after several generations to try setting a few free again in the wild. This is called reintroduction and has already brought some animals, like the Arabian oryx, back from extinction. Great care has to be taken to make sure the animals still know how to fend for themselves in the wild and do not rely on people for food. For reintroductions to work, the original reason for the animal's decline must no longer be a threat.

Reintroducing animals bred in captivity into the wild is one way to help endangered species. The Arabian oryx was killed off in the wild by hunters wanting its magnificent horns. But now captive-born herds have been successfully released in Oman where they are protected from hunting and disturbance. Hopefully, these animals will survive and breed in the wild.

CONSERVATION AND CONTROVERSY

Most people feel it's important to save wildlife, but sometimes conservation appears to interfere with other important things. If, for example, people make a living by cutting down trees, they may fear that the protection of an endangered species puts their jobs in jeopardy. Businesses making large profits from an industry may not want to change their practices in order to preserve species, either. Governments may become involved in resolving these issues. Because of such difficulties, saving wildlife is often not easy. The case of the northern spotted owl shows what can happen when conservation clashes with big businesses and the communities they employ.

Only 3,000 pairs of the northern spotted owl are left in the ancient forests along the Pacific coast of North America. Logging is destroying the owl's habitat, and if it continues, the owl will soon be extinct. Timber companies and loggers believe that cutting trees brings needed money to the Pacific Northwest. Conservationists want to halt logging to protect the owl, other wildlife, and the old-growth forests themselves. The U.S. government has approved limited logging, so devastation of the forests continues, as does the controversy.

Saving habitats

Most conservationists agree that the single most important thing that can be done to save the world's wildlife is to preserve natural habitats. Wild animals cannot survive without them anyway, and by saving a habitat a number of animal and plant species can be helped at the same time.

One of the best ways to do this is to turn a natural landscape into a reserve—a place set aside for nature. Inside a reserve, habitat destruction should either be kept to a minimum or not allowed at all. A reserve can also be a refuge from hunters, and one of the jobs of the people who run a reserve is to guard it from harmful intruders.

Today there are many thousands of reserves around the world protecting forests, grasslands, deserts, mountains, wetlands, seashores, and coral reefs. They range in size from tiny sanctuaries of a few acres, perhaps protecting a single marsh or a patch of woodland, to giant national parks covering thousands of square miles where a variety of different habitats are preserved.

Some reserves have been set up by individual people—in fact, some of the oldest ones were parts of estates set aside by landowners as places where they could hunt deer and game for sport. Others have been set up by charities devoted to conservation such as the World Wildlife Fund. Many of the biggest are run by governments, which usually have a department responsible for wildlife and national parks.

Some reserves are strictly the home of wildlife and few people are allowed to go inside. Others, especially the big national parks, may have communities living and working in them and they can attract lots of tourists. If so, their impact on the habitat and any disturbance of wildlife needs to be carefully controlled.

Unfortunately, many reserves and national parks are not protected well enough. Guards and rangers cannot always stop intruders from coming into reserves to poach animals. Also, governments

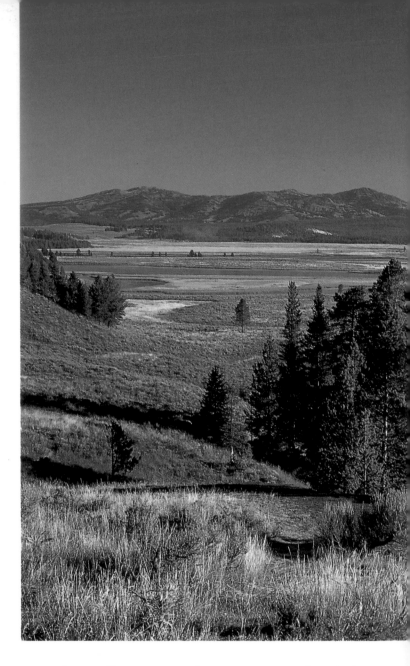

sometimes allow companies to cut trees for timber or to dig mines inside national parks as a way of raising money. Natural landscapes are always popular with tourists, and if a reserve is home for spectacular animals, such as gorillas, bears, or flocks of beautiful parrots, visitors will come and see them and pay an admission fee which may profit the reserve. Great care has to be taken, however, that the number of visitors does not harm the reserve or its inhabitants.

But even good reserves are not enough to save the great variety of wildlife on our planet well into the future. Less than 4 percent of all the world's land is protected. If the remaining 96 percent became suitable only for humans to live in we would lose countless numbers of species. Reserves are very

Yellowstone, the world's oldest national park (left) is also one of the largest. It covers 3,440 square miles of mountains, forests, meadows, lakes, and canyons in the western United States. Though many people visit the park, great efforts are made to ensure that they do as little damage as possible to the park's wildlife habitats. As a result, the park is a huge, safe home for animals such as bald eagles, grizzly bears, bighorn sheep, and American bison.

Conserving habitats helps wildlife everywhere, even in crowded cities. In many urban areas people have removed trash and dug ponds to help turn waste ground into attractive refuges for a variety of animals from butterflies to foxes (below). A thoughtfully planted garden can also attract wildlife and even the tiniest pond can make a home for dragonflies and frogs.

important for saving the best bits of wilderness that are left, but we must also find ways of letting wildlife continue to live alongside us.

There are various things that can be tried. Timber companies, for example, can cut down and remove trees in ways that do not destroy whole forests. Trees can be replanted where they used to grow and better methods can be found of getting rid of our waste so that it does not pollute rivers.

More and more people realize the importance of doing something for wildlife now before it is too late. In 1992, governments from all over the world met in Rio de Janeiro, Brazil, to discuss the future of our planet. One of the things they agreed on was the need for wealthy countries to help others protect their plants and animals.

North America and the Caribbean

Efforts to save wildlife from extinction started more than a century ago in North America.

People were worried about the future of North America's wildlife as long ago as 1872, when the famous Yellowstone National Park was established. At that time birds were hunted so ruthlessly that some, such as the passenger pigeon, became extinct. Other animals, such as buffalo, were shot in huge numbers on the prairies.

Since then, the continent's wildlife has faced even greater dangers because its natural habitats are being destroyed. Today, most of the rolling prairie is used for farmland. Two-thirds of the tropical forests of Central America have been cut down to make way for plantations and farms. Pine forests are being stripped away by logging companies.

Pollution has made many traditional habitats difficult places to live. The Great Lakes of Canada and the United States have been so badly polluted by waste from the cities around their shores that many animals have died. Sewage and oil have killed large stretches of coral in the Caribbean Sea.

But help is at hand. There are now controls on hunting and pollution. Hundreds of nature reserves like Yellowstone have been established. And in Central America, people are replanting tropical forests on unused farm plots.

Bald eagles became rare because they fed on fish contaminated with the chemical DDT. This made their eggshells so thin that few hatched safely. Now DDT is banned, the eagle population is recovering.

16

Problems in North America and the Caribbean

Endangered species in North America and the Caribbean have declined for many reasons. Environmental destruction for agriculture and industry, pollution, and hunting have all damaged wildlife and its habitats. The cougar, for example, has become extremely rare in many regions because its hunting grounds have been turned into fields or settlements. And although it seldom attacks farm animals—its usual prey is deer and smaller wild animals—farmers often kill it, thinking that will protect their herds. The West Indian manatee is in danger all round the Caribbean. It lives in estuaries and on coasts, often where people are busily using the water. Lots of manatees die every year when they collide with motor boats, become entangled in fishing nets, and are harmed by pollution.

The volcano rabbit lives only on the grassy slopes of a few high volcanoes near Mexico City. But farmers' fields are advancing uphill and taking over its home, and people hunt the rabbits for food. Hunting for food has also made the Central American river turtle rare.

1 Blue-headed quail dove

6 Volcano rabbit

18

7 American bison

② Central American river turtle

③ West Indian manatee

People say its meat tastes like chicken breast.

One of the most serious problems in tropical countries is the rapid disappearance of forests. Lots of animals that live in them cannot survive anywhere else. The blue-headed quail dove forages on the floor of tall, shady forests where there is not too much undergrowth. But on Cuba, where it lives, old, untouched forest like this is rare.

Finding money for conservation is not easy in the poorer countries around the Caribbean. But in the north there have been some famous success stories. The American bison, which was almost wiped out by hunting, has been carefully protected this century in places like the Yellowstone and Wood Buffalo national parks. Now there are more than a hundred thousand of them.

The last wild Californian condors were captured in 1987 to save them from the risk of being shot, poisoned, or accidentally killed. Since then the surviving birds have bred so well in zoos that two have been set free again. Conservationists hope to release more condors back into the wild soon.

⑤ Cougar

④ Californian condor

19

Spotted salamander

Spotted salamanders spend most of their time well out of sight burrowing through damp soil, but every spring they gather in writhing crowds around pools to mate and lay eggs in the water. Sadly, this spectacle no longer occurs in many areas because air pollution is creating acid rain. Dangerous chemicals then spill into the breeding pools and kill both eggs and young salamanders.

FOUND IN:	MAIN THREATS:	SCIENTIFIC NAME:	SIZE:
Eastern North America	**Pollution**	*Ambystoma maculatum*	6–10 in long

Cuban solenodon

The Cuban solenodon emerges at night to sniff out and snatch worms and insects from the forest floor. It is now rare—it has been attacked by introduced predators such as cats and mongooses, and has suffered from the clearance of trees. Three of the areas in which it lives have been turned into nature reserves.

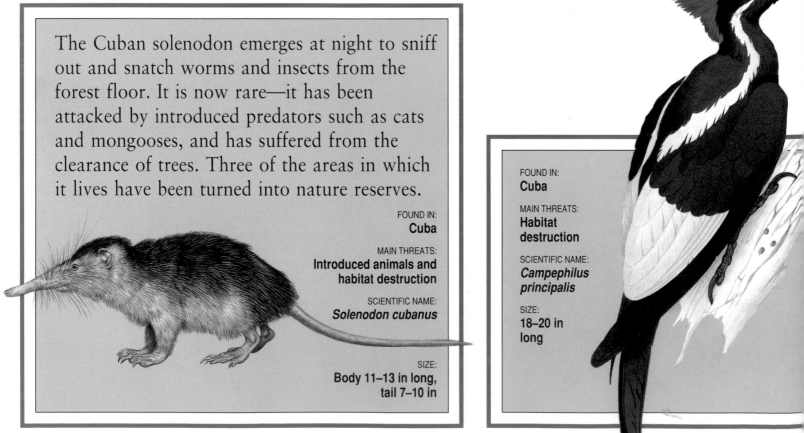

FOUND IN:
Cuba

MAIN THREATS:
Introduced animals and habitat destruction

SCIENTIFIC NAME:
Solenodon cubanus

SIZE:
Body 11–13 in long, tail 7–10 in

FOUND IN:
Cuba

MAIN THREATS:
Habitat destruction

SCIENTIFIC NAME:
Campephilus principalis

SIZE:
18–20 in long

Ingraham's hutia

FOUND IN:
Bahamas

SCIENTIFIC NAME:
Capromys ingrahami

SIZE:
14 ½ –15 ½ in long

MAIN THREATS:
Natural disasters, disease, and introduced animals

Once widespread in the Bahamas, Ingraham's hutia now thrives only on the small island of East Plana Cay, where several thousand of these large plant-eating rodents make colonies among the caves and rocks. This puts the whole population at risk from a natural disaster such as a hurricane, a fierce fire or a disease, or from predators such as cats. Just in case, a few hutias are now kept safely in captivity.

Ivory-billed woodpecker

This striking woodpecker can only survive in large stretches of old, undisturbed woodland. Many years of forest felling have therefore driven it close to extinction. Today, only a few remain in a remote pine forest reserve in eastern Cuba. There may also be some in the dense swamp forests of Louisiana or Florida, although the last definite sighting in the United States was in 1946.

Resplendent quetzal

This beautiful bird, with its shimmering plumage and long tail streamers, lives in the cloudy mountain forests that run from southern Mexico to Panama. Every year, more and more of these forests are cut down to make way for farming. Even where forests still exist, the quetzal is disappearing from the wild because local people catch so many to keep in cages as pets or to sell.

FOUND IN:
Central America

MAIN THREATS:
Habitat destruction and capture

SCIENTIFIC NAME:
Pharomachrus mocinno

SIZE:
Body 12 in long, tail streamers 15–30 in

Focus on: *Kemp's ridley turtle*

All the world's sea turtles are threatened by hunting, but Kemp's ridley has come closest to extinction. In the past, huge numbers of female turtles used to come ashore together to lay their eggs on the long sandy beach at Rancho Nuevo in Mexico. In 1947 as many as 40,000 turtles crowded on the sand during one mass nesting. But this amazing sight was not to last for long. More and more local people started to hunt the turtles and dig up their eggs from the beach, either to feed their families or to sell the meat and eggs in markets. Lots of these people were poor and hungry, but they took so many that the turtles began to disappear fast.

Soon only a few hundred turtles were left. By 1989 the total number of turtles coming ashore at any one time had plunged below four hundred. Today, hunting is banned and efforts are being made to protect the Kemp's ridley turtle but its future is still uncertain.

Every turtle counts
Though lots of people want to save sea turtles, Kemp's ridley is still in great danger. Today the main threats to the turtles are accidental. The turtles feed on crabs, shrimp, and fish on the seabed and many are caught in the nets used to catch these creatures.

SEA TURTLE
HOT-LINE
Please call with
Information
on
INJURED, MARKED
or STRANDED
SEA TURTLES

FLORIDA 1·800·432·6404
SOUTHEAST U.S. 1·800·327·6545

PUERTO RICO
& U.S. VIRGIN ISLANDS
(call direct) 1 305 350 7310

SOUTHEASTERN U.S. MARINE MAMMAL
AND SEA TURTLE STRANDING AND SALVAGE NETWORK
SPONSORED BY THE U.S. NATIONAL MARINE FISHERIES SERVICE/NOAA/DEPT. OF COMMERCE

LIVE SEA TURTLE
REPORTS ALSO WANTED

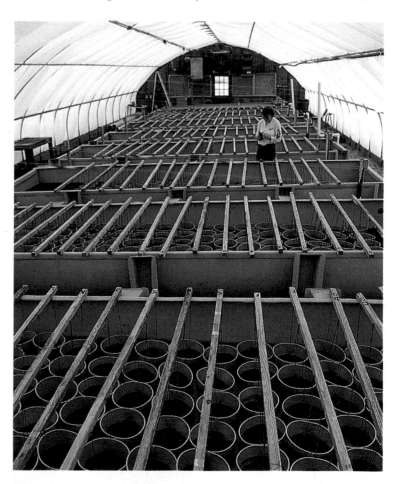

Getting a head start

To give Kemp's ridley as much chance as possible to recover, thousands of baby turtles are reared in special hatcheries in Texas and Mexico before being released into the sea. Captive breeding programs have been problematic, however, and the long-term success of these measures is still uncertain.

The hazards of nesting

Every year, between April and July, Kemp's ridley turtles lay their eggs on a single stretch of beach in Mexico. In the past, people used to lie in wait for them, ready to steal the eggs and kill the turtles as they slowly hauled themselves back toward the sea. Now there are special armed patrols on the beach to protect the nesting turtles from poachers.

Black-footed ferret

FOUND IN:
Central United States

MAIN THREATS:
Extermination of prey and disease

SCIENTIFIC NAME:
Mustela nigripes

SIZE:
**Body 15–18 in long,
tail 5–6 in**

When ranchers began killing prairie dogs to protect cattle range, the black-footed ferret seemed doomed. Starved by the disappearance of its prey, prone to disease, and accidentally poisoned, it nearly died out altogether. In 1986, the last few wild ferrets were rounded up, but since then they have bred so well in captivity that there are now about 300. Some are being returned to the wild.

FOUND IN:
Western Mexico

MAIN THREATS:
Capture

SCIENTIFIC NAME:
Brachypelma smithii

SIZE:
Up to 7 in legspan

Pronghorn

There may once have been over 40 million pronghorns grazing the American prairies. Hunting brought this number crashing down to fewer than 20,000 by the 1920s. Strict protection came just in time, and today the population has increased to almost half a million in the United States. But in Mexico pronghorns are still in danger from hunters and the loss of their habitat to cattle.

FOUND IN:
Western North America

MAIN THREATS:
Hunting and habitat destruction

SCIENTIFIC NAME:
Antilocapra americana

SIZE:
3–5 ft long

Red-kneed tarantula

This impressive spider lives in burrows in the dry lands of Mexico. Colorful, docile, and harmless to people, it is becoming a popular, exotic pet. Local people are starting to collect so many for export to the United States and Europe that the spiders could soon become very scarce in the wild. Conservationists say there should be much stronger controls on this trade.

Eskimo curlew

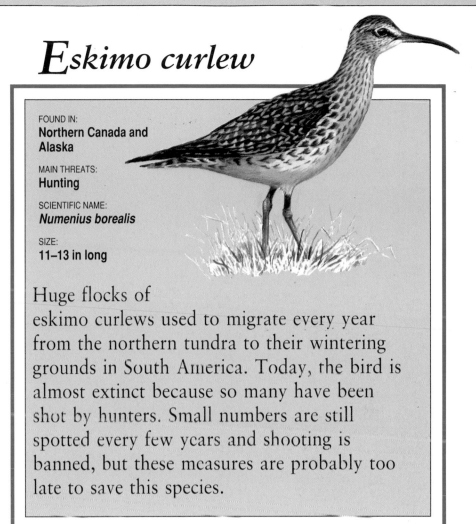

FOUND IN:
Northern Canada and Alaska

MAIN THREATS:
Hunting

SCIENTIFIC NAME:
Numenius borealis

SIZE:
11–13 in long

Huge flocks of eskimo curlews used to migrate every year from the northern tundra to their wintering grounds in South America. Today, the bird is almost extinct because so many have been shot by hunters. Small numbers are still spotted every few years and shooting is banned, but these measures are probably too late to save this species.

Rhinoceros iguana

This lizard, which gets its name from the pointed scales on its snout, lives only on Hispaniola and its small neighbor, Mona Island. Its future is threatened by the spread of villages and farms and by the various animals that have been brought to the islands. Donkeys and goats browse and trample on the scrubby vegetation in which it hides, and pigs, dogs, cats, and mongooses eat its eggs and attack its young.

FOUND IN:	MAIN THREATS:	SCIENTIFIC NAME:	SIZE:
West Indies	Habitat destruction and introduced animals	*Cyclura cornuta*	Up to 4 ft long

Gray whale

For more than 300 years, gray whales were at the mercy of whaling ships. They disappeared from the North Atlantic as early as the seventeenth century, and even now number fewer than 200 in the entire western Pacific. As a result of careful protection, the population in the eastern Pacific has increased to 21,000. These whales make a round-trip migration of 12,000 miles every year between the cold waters off the coast of Alaska, where they spend the summer, and the subtropical shores of Mexico, their winter home.

Queen conch

Divers collect this giant shellfish in shallow waters all around the Caribbean, both for local food markets and for shipping abroad. Such heavy fishing has placed a great strain on the species, and it is becoming increasingly rare in many areas.

FOUND IN:	MAIN THREATS:	SCIENTIFIC NAME:	SIZE:
Caribbean Sea and neighboring waters	Overfishing	*Strombus gigas*	Up to 8 ½ in long

Whooping crane

In 1941, there were fewer than 20 whooping cranes left in the wild, due to hunting and the drainage of their marshland habitats. Since then, strict hunting bans, protection of nesting and wintering sites, captive breeding, and even the use of other wild cranes as foster parents for chicks, has gradually built up the number to 140 in the wild. Nevertheless, the whooping crane is still in danger of extinction.

FOUND IN.
Northern Pacific Ocean

MAIN THREATS:
Hunting

SCIENTIFIC NAME:
Eschrichtius robustus

SIZE:
35–46 ft long

American alligator

FOUND IN:
**Northern Canada
and southern
United States**

MAIN THREATS:
**Habitat destruction
and hunting**

SCIENTIFIC NAME:
Grus americana

SIZE:
4–4 ½ ft long

Efforts to conserve the American alligator have been very successful and some people believe it is no longer endangered. Earlier this century the alligators were close to extinction because hunters killed so many for their skins which were made into shoes, belts, and purses. With hunting banned, there are now at least 800,000 alligators in the wild.

FOUND IN:
**Southeastern United
States**

MAIN THREATS:
Hunting

SCIENTIFIC NAME:
Alligator mississippiensis

SIZE:
6–19 ft long

South America

The wild landscapes of South America are changing fast. Even the world's greatest rain forest is in danger.

Three-quarters of South America is still covered by woodland, forest, savanna, or desert, and is teeming with fascinating wildlife. Today, however, this wilderness is threatened more and more.

Because the population is growing and land is scarce, people are forced into the wild to find new farming plots. Piece by piece the wilderness is disappearing. Those who settle there go into the surrounding habitats to hunt animals. They hunt for food, or for skins to sell, but also to capture monkeys or parrots to sell as pets.

All these activities are dangerous for wildlife. Many of the animals that live in the Andes Mountains are threatened by hunting and the spread of pasture. In the lowland savannas, grazing by cattle has made the grass too short to hide animals like the pampas deer.

But the greatest problems are in the rain forests. In the great Amazon forest, ranchers, settlers, logging companies, and huge industrial projects are destroying one of the richest wildlife habitats on earth. In the 1980s, about 8,500 square miles of forest were burned away every year. This is about the same area as Brazil's Jau National Park, one of several reserves in the Amazon. These protected areas will become even more important for the future safety of South America's natural landscapes and animal and bird life.

The golden lion tamarin has lost almost all of its rain forest habitat and more than half of these animals alive today are in zoos. Some of them are now being released into protected areas of the forest.

28

Problems in South America

Most endangered animals in South America are at risk for two reasons. Large parts of their habitat are being destroyed; and people hunt the animals in large numbers where their habitat does remain. The jaguar, for example, which needs big areas of rain forest in which to find enough prey, no longer has enough space in many areas because so much forest has been cut down. If it appears near settlements, hunters may kill it for its fur.

But rain forests are not the only habitats being destroyed. Animals in other areas are declining as well. The piglike Chaco peccary lives in drier, thorny forests, but these, too, are being cleared fast to make way for crops and cattle. Hunters, meanwhile, find peccaries easy to shoot for their meat because they bunch together when in danger.

Drained marshes and straightened, blocked, and polluted rivers have become unsuitable for the broad-nosed caiman. This small crocodile has also been hunted heavily for its hide.

Animals with low populations or very specialized needs are always at risk. The indigo macaw lives in a dry area of northeastern Brazil, where its main food is the nut of one particular type of palm. The spread of cattle farming has made the palms hard to find. To make things worse, people sometimes catch these lovely parrots and send them to

① White uakari

⑦ Jaguar

⑥ Hooded grebe

30

2 Broad-nosed caiman

collectors overseas. Now only about sixty of them remain in the wild. Animals with small ranges, like the white uakari, are also in danger. This unusual monkey is confined to a tiny area of rain forest. Since its color makes it a noticeable target, it can easily be killed off by hunters. There are probably only about five thousand hooded grebes left in Patagonia. These could be vulnerable if more people settle in their habitat.

The jaguar and the indigo macaw are protected by nature reserves in parts of their range, but it is hard to make these places completely safe. The vicuna, a relative of the camel, has had better luck. By 1965, out of an original population of several million, only six thousand vicunas remained in the Andes mountains. But since then, with careful protection against poachers in special reserves, their numbers have risen to about ninety thousand.

3 Indigo macaw

4 Vicuna

5 Chaco peccary

31

Woolly spider monkey

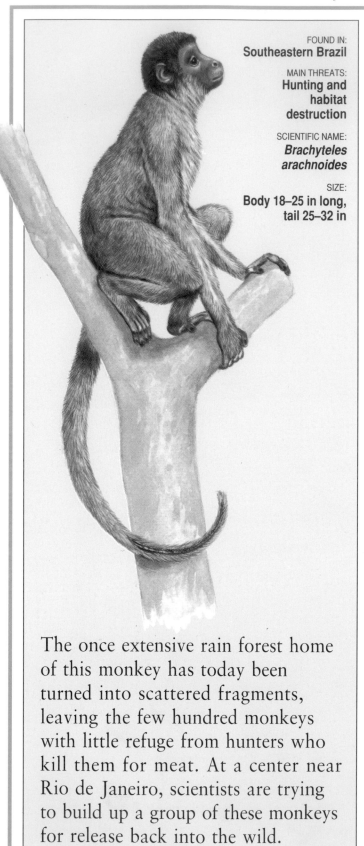

FOUND IN:
Southeastern Brazil

MAIN THREATS:
Hunting and habitat destruction

SCIENTIFIC NAME:
Brachyteles arachnoides

SIZE:
Body 18–25 in long, tail 25–32 in

The once extensive rain forest home of this monkey has today been turned into scattered fragments, leaving the few hundred monkeys with little refuge from hunters who kill them for meat. At a center near Rio de Janeiro, scientists are trying to build up a group of these monkeys for release back into the wild.

Toucan barbet

FOUND IN:
Colombia and Ecuador

MAIN THREATS:
Capture and habitat destruction

SCIENTIFIC NAME:
Semnornis ramphastinus

SIZE:
8 in long

This lively, colorful bird has become a popular pet in recent years. Trappers travel into the mountain forests to find it, and so many have been taken from the wild that it is now scarce. It is also running out of places to hide as the forest is cleared for farmland.

Marvelous spatuletail

Only the male spatuletail has these elaborate outer tail feathers. He uses them to try and impress a female by bending them forward and flying to and fro in front of her. Not a great deal is known about this remarkable bird. It seems to live only in the mountain forests of a small area of northern Peru—perhaps just a single valley. This means that the whole population is highly vulnerable to any changes in its habitat.

Emperor tamarin

Small troops of emperor tamarins dart through the trees looking for insects, fruit, tender leaves, and even flowers to eat. These monkeys are rare in the western Amazon, and their numbers are likely to fall further still as stretches of forest disappear to make way for ranches. Their best chance of survival is in protected areas such as Peru's Manu National Park.

FOUND IN:
Western Brazil, Peru, Bolivia

SCIENTIFIC NAME:
Saguinus imperator

MAIN THREATS:
Habitat destruction

SIZE:
Body 7–8 in long, tail 10–12 in

Giant armadillo

The giant armadillo weighs up to 130 pounds, and is a powerful digger. It can easily burrow into ants' nests and break open termite mounds to feed on the swarming insects. But because of its large size and tasty flesh, it is hunted in all areas where people also live. As more of its habitat disappears, its decline is sure to continue.

FOUND IN:
Northern Peru

MAIN THREATS:
Habitat destruction

SCIENTIFIC NAME:
Loddigesia mirabilis

SIZE:
Body 4–5 in long, tail up to 7 in

FOUND IN:
Venezuela to northern Argentina

SCIENTIFIC NAME:
Priodontes maximus

MAIN THREATS:
Hunting and habitat destruction

SIZE:
Body 2 ½–3 ft long, tail 16–20 in

Focus on: *Hyacinth macaw*

It is easy to see why the hyacinth macaw is highly prized by bird collectors. It not only has gorgeous plumage, but at up to three feet long is also the longest of all the parrots. Pet traders can sell it for well over $10,000 in Europe or North America. But in the end, the beauty of this tropical bird has been its downfall.

Flocks of hyacinth macaws used to live all over the drier regions of Brazil, Bolivia, and Paraguay. They started to decline because they were hunted for their meat and feathers, and because farmers cut down many of their nesting and feeding trees. Since the 1960s, the greed of the pet trade has made things much worse. So many wild macaws have been trapped and sent abroad that there are now only about three thousand left in all South America. They have completely disappeared from some areas. No more birds caught in the wild are supposed to be sold (only ones that have been bred in captivity), but with big money at stake, smugglers are always ready to break the law.

Six macaws head overseas
Each year, several hundred hyacinth macaws are taken illegally out of South America. Although most countries have laws to control the trade, people still smuggle wild-caught parrots across seas and borders. The birds are often sent in bad, cramped conditions with little food or water.

Nest robbing
The hyacinth macaw is one of several South American parrots that are seriously endangered because of capture for the cage bird trade. Trappers catch adult macaws and climb trees to steal chicks from the nests.

Spreading the message
Projects such as this painting on a school wall in Africa are important ways to help get local people interested in conservation. Colorful signs have been put up in parts of Brazil urging people not to harm the country's beautiful hyacinth macaw.

Spectacled bear

Pampas deer

The only bear in South America, this species takes its name from the white marks that ring its eyes. It dwells in wooded and open country high in the Andes Mountains, but is becoming increasingly scarce because these places are being cleared for farmland. It is also at risk because it sometimes raids corn crops and attacks farm animals, so farmers shoot it on sight.

FOUND IN:
Venezuela to Bolivia

MAIN THREATS:
Hunting and habitat destruction

SCIENTIFIC NAME:
Tremarctos ornatus

SIZE:
5–6 ft long

Chaco tortoise

Hunting for sport, food, and skins greatly reduced the numbers of pampas deer in South America. From 1860 to 1870, over two million skins were exported from Argentina alone. By 1975 that country had just 100 deer left. Today, with careful protection, there are now several hundred, but the deer will never recover fully because farms and cattle ranches have taken away the vast expanses of tall grass in which they once roamed.

FOUND IN:
Southern Brazil to northern Argentina

MAIN THREATS:
Hunting and habitat destruction

SCIENTIFIC NAME:
Ozotoceros bezoarticus

SIZE:
3 ½–4 ft long

The Chaco tortoise roams across dry, thorny ground, chewing fruit, grass, and cactus pads. Today it is in great peril because many thousands have been captured and smuggled abroad as pets,

Fluminense swallowtail

This beautiful butterfly is one of Brazil's most endangered insects. Drainage of its swampy, bushy habitat to build houses and factories and to lay out banana plantations has caused it to die out in many sites. Even the ten or so areas in which it still lives are under threat. Conservationists hope to be able to catch some butterflies and establish new colonies in safer places.

FOUND IN:
Southeastern Brazil

MAIN THREATS:
Habitat destruction

SCIENTIFIC NAME:
Parides ascanius

SIZE:
3 in wingspan

mainly to the United States. To save the wild population, the laws that are supposed to control this trade need to be enforced more strictly.

FOUND IN:
Paraguay and northern Argentina

MAIN THREATS:
Capture and hunting

SCIENTIFIC NAME:
Geochelone chilensis

SIZE:
Up to 14 in long

Northern screamer

FOUND IN:
Colombia and Venezuela

MAIN THREATS:
Hunting

SCIENTIFIC NAME:
Chauna chavaria

SIZE:
**29–35 in
long**

Although related to ducks and geese, the northern screamer does not have webbed feet like them, and seldom swims in open water. This noisy bird is restricted to the rivers and swamps of a small area in the north of South America. Here it walks around over floating leaves, its long toes helping to spread its weight. Since it has a small population, it is vulnerable to hunters who sometimes kill it for food.

Arrau river turtle

This turtle's habit of gathering in great numbers to lay its eggs on sandy riverbanks has led to its downfall. In the past, and still today, huge numbers of adults were killed and their eggs collected for food and oil. On some nesting beaches, millions of eggs were stolen every year. Now a few of the beaches are specially protected and the eggs are placed in pens in which the young can hatch in safety.

FOUND IN:
Amazon and Orinoco river systems

MAIN THREATS:
Hunting

SCIENTIFIC NAME:
Podocnemis expansa

SIZE:
23–35 in long

Spectacled caiman

FOUND IN:
Northern South America

MAIN THREATS:
Hunting

SCIENTIFIC NAME:
Caiman crocodilus

SIZE:
5–8 ft long

Boto

This freshwater dolphin still swims in the Amazon and Orinoco rivers. However, the effects of dams which block the rivers, forest clearance on the banks, and pollution from pesticides and factory chemicals may all reduce the amount of fish it has to eat. Botos also get caught accidentally in fish nets.

FOUND IN:
Amazon and Orinoco river systems

MAIN THREATS:
Habitat disruption and pollution

SCIENTIFIC NAME:
Inia geoffrensis

SIZE:
6 ½–10 ft long

Pirarucu

The pirarucu is one of the biggest freshwater fish in the world. A fierce hunter, it cruises through shallow water looking for prey. It has become rare in many areas because of fishing for its flesh (sometimes rifles and even dynamite are used to kill it), and large numbers of young have been caught for the aquarium trade.

FOUND IN:
Amazon river system

MAIN THREATS:
Overfishing

SCIENTIFIC NAME:
Arapaima gigas

SIZE:
Up to 10 ft long

The fate of the spectacled caiman hangs on the changing demand for crocodile skin. Millions used to be killed for their hide every year, especially in Colombia and Peru where numbers have declined dramatically. Today, fashion has turned against this trade, but poaching of caimans still continues and could easily rise again if enough people want to buy crocodile-skin products.

Africa

Two hundred years ago, Africa was teeming with wildlife. Today, many of its animals are at risk.

Africa's broad plains and dense forests were once full of wildlife. But when Europeans began to settle the continent in the nineteenth century, things started to change. More and more farms were built on the plains. Trees were cut down to make way for gardens and plantations. Before long, Africa's wildlife was in great danger.

The settlers' favorite sport was hunting. Soon they had killed millions of antelopes, zebras, giraffes, rhinoceroses, lions, and leopards. Pushed from their old homes and hunted, African animals started to decrease in number.

Today the threats to wildlife are greater still. Africa's population is growing by more than twenty million people every year, most of whom are poor. They need more space for their farms, roads, and settlements. There are too many cattle on the grasslands, and the forests are shrinking, but the deserts are growing. On the island of Madagascar, the forest is disappearing so fast that there may be almost none left in thirty years' time. Since most of Madagascar's species live only in this forest, it would mean the extinction of hundreds of species.

Africa and Madagascar now have many reserves and national parks where some animals can live in safety. Parks such as the Serengeti (Tanzania), Masai Mara (Kenya), Kruger (South Africa), Kafue (Zambia), and Tai (Ivory Coast) attract thousands of visitors every year.

The mountain gorilla has long been at risk from hunters who invade its misty highland home. Now it is strictly protected and tourists coming to see it in the wild help pay for its conservation.

Problems in Africa

As Africa's human population grows and agricultural needs expand, its wildlife is gradually running out of space. Many of the wild grazing animals, for example, are being forced to leave the plains as cattle take over the pasture. Predatory animals such as the brown hyena may then try to catch livestock when they cannot find their natural prey. This puts them at risk from farmers. In southern Africa so many hyenas have been shot that they are now rarely seen outside reserves.

As with several unusual animals of South America's rain forests, many African animals are specifically adapted to a particular habitat and find survival difficult if their environment is disturbed. Huge areas of Africa's great rain forests have already been destroyed. This is a big threat to all the animals of the forest, especially to those that live in only a few areas. The white-necked rockfowl nests only in caves and on rocky cliffs surrounded by dense rain forest, but good sites are becoming hard to find. Madagascar's forests are being cleared so fast that twenty-six out of the thirty types of lemur on the island are threatened. This includes the indri, which is the biggest species.

⑥

③

⑤

④

②

⑦

⑦ Bontebok

⑥ White-necked rockfowl

42

② Brown hyena

③ Nile crocodile

④ Indri

Hunting for food and poaching for skins, horns, and tusks are great threats to many animals already suffering because their habitats are being destroyed. From 1950 to 1980 at least three million Nile crocodiles were killed for their skins. Although the black rhinoceros is protected by armed guards, it is still not safe from poachers, even in national parks. There are only a few thousand left in Africa.

The bontebok was ruthlessly hunted, but it was saved from extinction just in time. Reserves were created in the few areas of South Africa where it survived and the numbers of bontebok are growing again. There have also been projects to return some African animals to the wild from captivity. Groups of Barbary macaques have been released in a few areas of north Africa, where they once lived.

⑤ Black rhinoceros

Ruffed lemur

FOUND IN:
Eastern Madagascar

MAIN THREATS:
Habitat destruction, hunting, and capture

SCIENTIFIC NAME:
Varecia variegata

SIZE:
Body 21–22 in long, tail 23–25 in

The ruffed lemur gets its name from the thick collar of fur around its neck. In the lush rain forest of eastern Madagascar, where it makes its home, groups of up to five lemurs may be seen clambering through the trees in search of fruit. But their home is no longer safe. Large areas of the forest are being cut down for farmland. In addition, some people hunt lemurs for food, while others take them away as pets.

Congo peacock

This shy, rare bird lives so deep in the African rain forest that scientists did not actually discover it until 1936 (they only knew it existed because a feather had been seen 23 years before). Even now, little is known about the Congo peacock's life in the wild, but because its numbers are already small, it is sure to suffer if more of the forest disappears.

FOUND IN:
Eastern Zaire

MAIN THREATS:
Habitat destruction

SCIENTIFIC NAME:
Afropavo congensis

SIZE:
24–28 in long

FOUND IN:
West Africa

MAIN THREATS:
Habitat destruction and hunting

SCIENTIFIC NAME:
Choeropsis liberiensis

SIZE:
5–6 ft long

Chimpanzee

There are fewer than 200,000 chimpanzees left in the wild. This sounds like a lot, but they are scattered over a large area and have disappeared from many places where their habitat has been destroyed. Hunting chimpanzees is against the law now but it still goes on. Some people kill the adults so that they can capture the young ones to sell abroad for medical experiments.

FOUND IN:
West and Central Africa

SCIENTIFIC NAME:
Pan troglodytes

MAIN THREATS:
Habitat destruction, hunting, and capture

SIZE:
25–37 in long

Aye-aye

FOUND IN:
Madagascar

SCIENTIFIC NAME:
Daubentonia madagascariensis

MAIN THREATS:
Habitat destruction and hunting

SIZE:
Body 14–17 in long, tail 16 in

The aye-aye uses its very long middle finger to pull insects out of tree bark. Local tradition says that this strange animal brings bad luck and for that reason it is often killed. Conservationists hope they can change these old beliefs and make people want to protect both the aye-aye and its forest home.

Pygmy hippopotamus

This small cousin of the well-known hippopotamus often lives around swamps, but it spends most of its time on dry land. It has become rare in all the places where it still lives. Most of its forest habitat has already been cut down and hunters kill the animal for its meat. Conservationists say that its numbers will fall dramatically unless it is given careful protection inside nature reserves.

45

Focus on: *African elephant*

The African elephant is one of the best loved of all animals, but this has not saved it from the hunter's gun. The elephant is at risk because of its ivory tusks. Ivory used to be sent all over the world and made into things like piano keys, carvings, and jewelry. Eventually laws were passed to control hunting. But ivory is now so valuable that poachers ignore the laws and even go deep into nature reserves in search of elephants to kill. During the 1980s the number of wild elephants in all of Africa crashed faster than ever, from 1.3 million in 1979 down to about 600,000 by 1990.

Only drastic action could save the elephant, so in 1989 most countries agreed to ban all trade in ivory. Poaching declined after this. Now some African countries want to start selling ivory legally again, but a lot of other countries would like to keep the ban until the elephant population has had a better chance to recover.

Dustbathing in safety
In well-guarded reserves there is much less poaching, and elephant herds are fairly safe. But reserves are of limited size and a few in southern Africa are even said to be overcrowded.

46

Prey to the gun

Gangs of elephant poachers are armed with rifles and machine guns. When they find a herd, they shoot as many as they can, then cut off all the ivory tusks. In the 1980s about 1,500 elephants were killed every week. Since the ban on ivory trading in 1989, the number killed by poachers has dropped in most areas.

Burning tusks

These tusks, worth millions of dollars, have been seized from poachers. By burning them, the Kenyan government has made sure they will not be sold or smuggled to ivory carvers in Asia. If shops stop buying ivory, elephants will be helped even more.

Hermit ibis

This peculiar bald-headed bird used to be much more widespread, but it does not cope well with changes in its habitat and food supply caused by farming. Last seen in Turkey in 1989, it now breeds only in Morocco, in a rather dry, rocky area where there is not much farming. Although the four nesting colonies there have increased slightly in size, the total wild population of 220 is still small.

FOUND IN:
Morocco

MAIN THREATS:
Habitat destruction

SCIENTIFIC NAME:
Geronticus eremita

SIZE:
28–31 in long

Pancake tortoise

This remarkable tortoise has a soft, flexible shell. If in danger, it can crawl into a rocky crevice and breathe in lots of air, making its body expand so much that it is stuck fast and very difficult to pull out. But this does not protect the animal from hunters who catch large numbers for the pet trade.

FOUND IN:
Kenya and Tanzania

MAIN THREATS:
Capture

SCIENTIFIC NAME:
Malocochersus tornieri

SIZE:
7 in long

Addax

The addax is one of the few large animals that live in the Sahara Desert. It feeds on desert plants and gets all the moisture it needs from them. It has been hunted near to extinction for sport and for its horns, and where it still lives cattle often trample on and destroy its food. Plans to release some captive addax into reserves may succeed, but only if people leave them in peace.

Grevy's zebra

Grevy's zebra is endangered because its beautiful, narrow-striped coat makes the animal a target for hunters who sell skins. The largest of all zebras, it roams across dry, sparsely wooded country from northern Kenya to Ethiopia. There are probably only three isolated populations left now, numbering about 15,000 animals in all.

FOUND IN:	MAIN THREATS:	SCIENTIFIC NAME:	SIZE:
East Africa	**Hunting and habitat destruction**	*Equus grevyi*	**Body 8 ft long, tail 20 in**

Hunting dog

FOUND IN:	MAIN THREATS:
North Africa	**Hunting and habitat destruction**
SCIENTIFIC NAME:	SIZE:
Addax nasomaculatus	**Body 4 ft long, tail 10–14 in**

Hunting dogs once stalked prey throughout the African savanna, but today they are found only in a few scattered places. Huge numbers of the dogs have been shot by farmers who believe they will attack their livestock. To survive, the dogs need large, wild areas of land with plenty of prey such as gazelles and zebras. Today, most places like this are in national parks.

FOUND IN:
Africa, south of the Sahara

MAIN THREATS:
Hunting and habitat destruction

SCIENTIFIC NAME:
Lycaon pictus

SIZE:
Body up to 3 ft long, tail 12–16 in

Madagascar fish eagle

With only about 30 nesting pairs left, this is one of the rarest of all birds. In the 1930s it was still quite common along the northwest coast of Madagascar, but since then it has declined dramatically, partly because it has been shot in some areas and its nests destroyed. It usually hunts around shallow estuaries and coastal swamps where it can plunge down to catch fish.

FOUND IN:	MAIN THREATS:	SCIENTIFIC NAME:	SIZE:
Northwest Madagascar	Hunting and disturbance	*Haliaeetus vociferoides*	27–31 in long

West African dwarf crocodile

This small crocodile has become rare in recent years because of changes to the rivers and lakes it inhabits and because of ruthless hunting. A slow-moving and not very dangerous animal, it is easy to kill or catch. Some people take it for its meat, but most want to sell its skin for money. There are even whole, stuffed animals on sale to tourists in some countries.

FOUND IN:	MAIN THREATS:	SCIENTIFIC NAME:	SIZE:
West and Central Africa	Hunting and habitat disruption	*Osteolaemus tetraspis*	5 ft long

Coelacanth

When a strange, deep-water fish was trawled up accidentally in a net in 1938, scientists realized that a group of fish known from ancient fossils still lived off the coast of Africa. Since then, about 100 coelacanths have been netted around the Comoro Islands near Madagascar. Because it is rare and seems to inhabit a small area, scientists fear for the survival of this "living fossil." Already traces of chemical pollution have been found in its body.

FOUND IN:
Indian Ocean, off southeast Africa

MAIN THREATS:
Pollution and overfishing

SCIENTIFIC NAME:
Latimeria chalumnae

SIZE:
up to 6 ft long

Allen's swamp monkey

This little-known monkey lives near rivers and in swamps. Though it eats mainly leaves and fruit, it also goes into the water to snatch crabs and even fish. It, in turn, is hunted by local people for meat and because it sometimes raids farmers' crops. Because it prefers waterside trees, the monkey is quite easy for hunters in boats to track down and shoot.

FOUND IN:
Congo and Zaire

SCIENTIFIC NAME:
Allenopithecus nigroviridis

MAIN THREATS:
Hunting

SIZE:
Body 16–20 in long, tail 18–21 in

51

Europe

In Europe's crowded landscape, any small area of unpolluted land has become a precious refuge for wildlife.

Europe was once almost completely covered by thick woodland. Today, the continent is crowded with people, farms, settlements, and roads; natural habitats are like islands in a sea of towns and cities. Animals that used to roam widely, such as bears, wild boars, wolves, storks, and eagles, have disappeared from most regions.

New opportunities for wildlife have been created—hedgerows, grazing meadows, and grouse moors are artificial habitats that have become homes to certain species. However, many of these are now threatened as farmers try to make their land more productive.

Europe's concentration of people, farmland, and industry brings other problems. Heavy pollution harms river and sea creatures. It also affects animals that feed on these creatures, such as the otter and the osprey. More than half the Mediterranean coastline is polluted by sewage. Hunters still threaten many animals: every year a total of 900 million birds are killed for sport as they migrate between Europe and Africa.

Fortunately, conservation efforts have helped many European animals. There are strong laws to protect wildlife and increasing controls on pollution. Each country has reserves and parks for wildlife. These protect areas of undamaged land and those that have been least disturbed by people, such as mountains and wetlands.

The large copper butterfly lives in fens and marshes—wetland areas that are becoming increasingly scarce because of land drainage for farming. This butterfly is extinct in Britain and rare all over Europe.

Problems in Europe

① Russian desman

As in North America and the Caribbean, all sorts of problems such as hunting, pollution, and destruction of habitats threaten wildlife across the densely populated countries of Europe. For instance, the barn owl was hunted so much by gamekeepers and sportsmen that it became scarce in Europe over a hundred years ago. Since then, many of the old trees and barns in which it nested have been removed. The owl is also poisoned by pesticides and is often killed by road traffic.

Similarly, the rare Russian desman was widely hunted in the rivers of western Russia for its soft fur. The desman also has to face water pollution, changing river levels, and the invasion of its habitat by muskrats and coypus that have escaped from farms where they are bred for their fur. These animals compete with the desman for space and food.

The starlet sea anemone, which lives in tidal pools, has also suffered because of pollution and because its pools have been cut off from the sea. It survives in just four places off the shores of southern England.

Some animals are still trying to recover from the time when hunting was at its most popular in the nineteenth century. During that time the hobby became very rare, mainly because gamekeepers

⑥ Hobby

54

② Wildcat

③ Barn owl

killed it and egg-collectors raided its nests. Today it is still scarce, even in places where hunting has stopped. The bowhead whale, which swims in the cold waters of the Arctic Ocean, was hunted almost to extinction by whalers. They stopped hunting this giant mammal long ago, but very few have been seen since in the seas near Europe.

The loggerhead turtle, which lives in the Mediterranean Sea, has suffered because hotels and tourists have spoiled most of the beaches on which it used to lay its eggs. However, many people are now campaigning to save the turtle, and parts of some beaches have been turned into turtle sanctuaries.

Changing attitudes toward wildlife have already helped lots of animals in Europe. The wildcat was ruthlessly hunted in the past to protect game such as grouse and partridges, but far fewer people want to shoot or trap it today. As a result, the wildcat has increased in numbers and is returning to some forests and moors where it used to live.

④ Loggerhead turtle

⑤ Bowhead whale

Corncrake

FOUND IN:
Europe and western Asia

MAIN THREATS:
Habitat destruction and disturbance

SCIENTIFIC NAME:
Crex crex

SIZE:
10–12 in long

The corncrake used to thrive on farms, often nesting in the hayfields, but farms are now dangerous places to live. As more and more hedgerows are removed, weeds killed, and field edges tidied, the birds have fewer places to hide and find food. Hay-cutting machines ruin many nests and even kill adults and chicks. The corncrake is becoming rare in most countries.

Greater horseshoe bat

This bat roosts in caves, trees, and roofs of old buildings. But as caves are explored, trees felled, and buildings pulled down, homes are becoming harder to find. Many bats have been poisoned by chemicals used to preserve roof timber. This bat is almost extinct in northwestern Europe.

FOUND IN:
Europe, Asia, and North Africa

SCIENTIFIC NAME:
Rhinolophus ferrumequinum

MAIN THREATS:
Habitat destruction, disturbance, and poisoning

SIZE:
4 ½–5 in long

Spur-thighed tortoise

This tortoise comes from dry, scrubby regions around the Mediterranean Sea—places that are being changed by farming and the building of vacation apartments. It is rare because millions were captured and sold as pets. Some trade still goes on, but it is now banned by most countries to give the tortoises a chance to recover in the wild.

FOUND IN:
Southern Europe and North Africa

MAIN THREATS:
Capture and habitat destruction

SCIENTIFIC NAME:
Testudo graeca

SIZE:
Up to 10 in long

European bison

Like its American cousin, the European bison was hunted for its meat. Although it died out in the wild in 1919 there were still some animals in zoos. Six of these were set free in a safe part of Poland's Bialowieza forest. They bred and prospered, and now more than 250 European bison live wild in the forest again.

FOUND IN:	MAIN THREATS:	SCIENTIFIC NAME:	SIZE:
Eastern Europe	**Hunting**	*Bison bonasus*	**8–9 ft long**

Red kite

FOUND IN:
Western, southern, and eastern Europe

MAIN THREATS:
Hunting and capture

SCIENTIFIC NAME:
Milvus milvus

SIZE:
24–26 in long

The red kite was a common scavenger hundreds of years ago, before hunters destroyed huge numbers. Now fewer than fifty pairs survive in most countries, and it is rare enough for people to make money by stealing its eggs and young to sell. And illegal killing still goes on. In 1989, eleven kites were found poisoned in Wales, their only British nesting site.

Focus on: European otter

The otter has become rare in many parts of Europe, especially in lowland areas that have the most people, towns, farms, and factories. The worst problem the otter faces is pollution of the rivers, lakes, and marshes in which it hunts for fish and other water creatures. The first sign of this came in the l950s when otters declined rapidly in Britain. Studies showed they had been poisoned by powerful chemicals called organochlorine pesticides that farmers were using in sheep-dips and spraying on their crops. These washed into streams and passed to the otters through their food.

Most farmers stopped using these pesticides, but other kinds of pollution, including factory waste, continued to ruin rivers. Otters now no longer live in Switzerland, for example, because the rivers have been badly contaminated. Fortunately, lots of people want to save the otter. They hope that if rivers can be cleaned up and otter habitats conserved, the animal will one day return to some of its old homes.

The perils of dirty water
Otters are very sensitive to pollution. If they eat lots of fish that have been feeding in polluted rivers and lakes, dangerous chemicals quickly build up in their own bodies. Sometimes the otters eat so much polluted fish that they are poisoned to death. Or the chemicals they consume may make them unable or too unhealthy to breed. If the adults are no longer producing young, the otter population in a polluted area is doomed to die out.

Ideal home

Otters like rivers with plenty of plants growing on the
banks and mature overhanging trees under which they
can make their dens. Sadly, many riversides in lowland
Europe have been cleared and
old trees have been chopped down.
Helping otters to survive can
include replanting trees
along riverbanks and
providing artificial
dens made from
rocks or sticks.

Dalmatian pelican

FOUND IN:
**Southeastern
Europe to China**

MAIN THREATS:
**Habitat destruction
and hunting**

SCIENTIFIC NAME:
Pelecanus crispus

SIZE:
5–6 ft long

With the perfect bill for scooping up fish, it is not surprising that the Dalmatian pelican is the enemy of many fish-farmers. But because fish-farmers and fishermen shoot so many pelicans and because marshy habitats are being drained, farmed, or built over, this bird is now very rare. Millions of pelicans used to nest on the delta of the Danube River—now there are just 40 pairs there.

Medicinal leech

FOUND IN:
**Western,
southern, and
eastern Europe**

MAIN THREATS:
Capture

SIZE:
4–5 in long

SCIENTIFIC NAME:
**Hirudo
medicinalis**

Until this century, many doctors used leeches to remove blood from their patients as a way of treating some illnesses. Leeches normally suck blood from animals that wade into streams or ponds. Millions of them were taken from the wild every year, and they soon became scarce. Today, leeches are in demand again for the special substance they have that stops blood clotting.

FOUND IN:
**Mediterranean
Sea**

MAIN THREATS:
Pollution and hunting

SCIENTIFIC NAME:
Monachus monachus

SIZE:
6 ½–10 ft long

FOUND IN:
**European coastal
waters**

SCIENTIFIC NAME:
Acipenser sturio

MAIN THREATS:
**Overfishing and
habitat disruption**

SIZE:
3–10 ft long

Mediterranean monk seal

There are probably fewer than 500 of these seals left in the entire Mediterranean. They have been badly affected by pollution and many of their breeding grounds have been

wrecked by the tourist trade. The monk seals are also still hunted by fishermen who blame them for tearing open nets and snatching captured fish.

Common sturgeon

The common sturgeon spends most of its time foraging on the seabed, but every year it swims more than 300 miles inland to spawn. But dams and other obstructions have stopped its breeding in many rivers, and at sea huge numbers have been caught for food. A famous and expensive food called caviar is made of eggs taken from the female fish. Today, the sturgeon is scarce in most waters.

Olm

This strange salamander lives in the darkness of underground streams and lakes. There it rummages in the mud to find food. Animal collectors have taken so many of these fascinating creatures from the wild that new areas where they have been found are kept secret. Conservationists are also worried that the clean, crystal-clear water in which they swim may become polluted by factories.

FOUND IN:
Yugoslavia and Italy

SCIENTIFIC NAME:
Proteus anguinus

MAIN THREATS:
Capture and pollution

SIZE:
8–12 in long

Asia

Ruthless hunting and the destruction of natural habitats have put many of Asia's animals in danger.

With its huge size, varied landscape, and uneven spread of people, Asia poses different problems for wildlife in different regions. In the north and west, where few people live, many wild places for animals remain. However, hunting has endangered some larger creatures such as antelopes, deer, and big cats.

By contrast, in the crowded lands of the south and east, cultivation has changed much of the landscape. Grasslands have been thinned and large areas of forest have been cleared. In these parts, many animals now only survive in protected areas. Even when animals are officially protected they are not always safe. Poachers have continued to shoot Asian elephants, even those that live inside Thailand's Khao Yai National Park.

There are still large areas of tropical rain forest across the islands of Southeast Asia. But every year the increase in population and the actions of logging companies reduce the rain forest. At least 126 species of birds in Indonesia are endangered— the highest number for any country in the world.

Efforts are now being made to help the animals at risk. Animals are protected in national parks and reserves and by the work of environmentalists. The Chikpo protest movement in India has managed to stop some logging plans, for example. Meanwhile, conservation programs have saved animals such as the Arabian oryx from extinction.

Ten years after hunters killed the last wild Arabian oryx, the animals reappeared in the desert. Groups of oryx from zoos were carefully brought back to the wild and there are now about 100 roaming free.

62

Problems in Asia

(1) Indian python

The gradual spread of farms and settlements into wild habitats is the biggest problem for wildlife in Asia. It threatens some famous endangered animals. The giant panda, the symbol of the World Wildlife Fund, has lost most of the Chinese bamboo forests it once inhabited. Now fewer than one thousand pandas remain, scattered in small groups. The tiger has disappeared from many parts of south and east Asia. It needs a large area of forest in which to hunt, and quickly runs out of space if burning and felling damage its home. From six thousand to nine thousand wild tigers are left worldwide—in 1900 India alone had fifty thousand. Another big mammal, the leaf-eating Malayan tapir, is in great danger because of deforestation in Malaya and Sumatra.

Hunting, too, takes its toll on these animals. Poachers kill pandas and tigers to sell their valuable skins. Farmers shoot tapirs if they come out of the forest to raid crops. Hunting also threatens the Victoria crowned pigeon. At close to three feet in length, it is a giant among pigeons, and it provides plenty of tasty meat for people in the forests of New Guinea. The Indian python is a big, powerful

(6)

(7)

(3)

(2)

(1)

(4)

(6) Siberian white crane

(7) Onager

64

② Tiger

snake, capable of suffocating a leopard in its coils. But it, too, has disappeared from many regions—it has been ruthlessly hunted for its skin and captured for the pet trade.

In recent years there have been big efforts to conserve some of these spectacular animals. The Chinese government has promised to fund lots of new reserves for pandas. Helped by special refuges such as the Ranthambore Tiger Reserve, tigers have more than doubled in number in India since 1970. The onager, a type of wild ass from Iran, was hunted and pushed from good pasture and drinking water by farmers' herds. But its numbers are rising again and some animals that were raised in captivity have been released back into the wild.

The wild population of the rare Siberian white crane is just fourteen. Conservationists hope to increase the number by fooling other nesting cranes into acting as foster parents for the white crane's eggs. Some of the eggs they plan to use will have been laid by captive white cranes in the United States.

③ Giant panda

⑤

④ Malayan tapir

⑤ Victoria crowned pigeon

65

Pileated gibbon

The pileated gibbon uses its long arms to swing from branch to branch, high in forest trees. Tree clearing has taken away most of the mature forest it needs, and local people kill the animal for its meat. Once there were two to three million pileated gibbons in Thailand alone; now the total population is probably below 20,000.

FOUND IN:
Thailand, Cambodia, and Laos

MAIN THREATS:
Habitat destruction and hunting

SCIENTIFIC NAME:
Hylobates pileatus

SIZE:
18–24 in long

Helmeted hornbill

The thick lump on the helmeted hornbill's beak is made of solid ivory and is more valuable than elephant ivory. Ivory hunters have caused the bird to disappear from many areas. It is also badly affected by tree felling because each pair of birds needs a large area of forest in which to find food.

FOUND IN:
Malaysia, Borneo, and Sumatra

MAIN THREATS:
Hunting and habitat destruction

SCIENTIFIC NAME:
Rhinoplax vigil

SIZE:
Body up to 28 in long, tail up to 20 in

Sumatran rhinoceros

This is the smallest and hairiest of all the rhinoceroses. Its horn, which is ground to powder and used in traditional medicine, is very valuable and much sought after. There are now only a few hundred left and many of the forests in which they survive are being chopped down. This leaves small groups of rhinos marooned and even more at risk from poachers.

Queen Alexandra's birdwing

Ribbon-tailed bird of paradise

This giant butterfly is the biggest in the world. It is very valuable, so local people catch it to sell to traders. But if some of the forest in which the butterflies live can be saved in reserves, local people might be able to make money from tourism instead.

FOUND IN:
New Guinea

MAIN THREATS:
Habitat destruction and capture

SCIENTIFIC NAME:
Ornithoptera alexandrae

SIZE:
6–10 in wingspan

This amazing bird lives in a small part of the mountain forest, where it is still quite common. But it could be at risk in the future if the forest is destroyed. Only the male has the 3-foot-long tail ribbons, which he twitches excitedly when trying to impress a female. Until 1939 the bird was known only to local tribes who used its ribbons to decorate their headdresses.

FOUND IN:
Southeast Asia

MAIN THREATS:
Hunting and habitat destruction

SCIENTIFIC NAME:
Dicerorhinus sumatrensis

SIZE:
8–9 ft long

FOUND IN:
New Guinea

MAIN THREATS:
Hunting and habitat destruction

SCIENTIFIC NAME:
Astrapia mayeri

SIZE:
Body 12–14 in long, tail streamers up to 3 ft

Focus on: Orangutan

Nobody knows exactly how many orangutans there are living deep in the tropical rain forests of Sumatra and Borneo, but the number could now be as low as a few thousand. Every year, more and more of their forest home is cut down, mainly for timber. The shy orangutan cannot survive even selective logging, in which only the biggest trees are removed, because it can no longer move about easily from branch to branch in the forest canopy and find enough food.

Once the noise of tree felling begins, an orangutan will hide in another patch of forest. But the new area will be unfamiliar and the wandering ape may find itself trespassing on a neighbor's patch (each orangutan needs almost two square miles of forest to live in). The newcomer may not be able to find enough food. It is unlikely to breed if it cannot find enough space to live in. Young orangutans are also captured and traded illegally as pets or laboratory animals for medical experiments.

Home away from home

At forest sanctuaries such as the Sepilok Rehabilitation Center in Borneo, once-captive orangutans are given the chance to return to the wild. Many of these apes have been taken back from people trying to smuggle them overseas for sale. They are often in poor condition and need careful tending before they can be released back into the surrounding forest.

Fallen giants

Logging of rain forest trees for timber poses a huge threat, not just to orangutans, but to all the wildlife in Southeast Asian rain forests. Sumatra has already lost more than half its forests, and logging threatens some nature reserves.

Life in the trees

Orangutans spend most of their lives high in the rain forest canopy. They swing from branch to branch to feed on fruit by day and rest on nests of broken branches and leaves by night. Logging quickly ruins their home. It opens up gaps in the canopy, breaks the dangling creepers they use for climbing, and destroys necessary food plants such as creeping figs.

*S*now   leopard

There might be as many 5,000 snow leopards still living in the high mountains of central Asia. Although their home is so remote, the leopards are still pursued by hunters who shoot them for their beautiful fur, which is very valuable. Farmers also shoot the snow leopards because they sometimes attack herds of domestic cattle when they cannot find their normal prey—wild goats.

FOUND IN:	MAIN THREATS:	SCIENTIFIC NAME:	SIZE:
Central Asia	**Hunting**	***Panthera uncia***	**Body 4–5 ft long, tail 3–4 ft**

*C*heer pheasant

The cheer pheasant lives on steep, grassy slopes up to 10,000 feet high in the Himalayas. It is one of many Asian pheasants that are in danger. Grazing herds and fires set by farmers have ruined much of the grass it likes, and it is widely hunted for food—even inside nature reserves. It has already become extinct in Pakistan and is rare now in most countries.

FOUND IN:	MAIN THREAT:
Himalayas	**Habitat destruction and hunting**
SCIENTIFIC NAME:	SIZE:
Catreus wallichii	**2–4 ft long**

Komodo dragon

Imagine a lizard ten feet long and strong enough to kill a deer! The Komodo dragon is a frightening lizard and is sometimes shot because it is known to attack or kill farm animals and even people. But it is also a big tourist attraction. It is specially protected on Komodo and the few islands where it lives and conservationists hope that the 7,500 lizards that are left will be safe.

FOUND IN:
Indonesia

MAIN THREATS:
Hunting

SCIENTIFIC NAME:
Varanus komodoensis

SIZE:
Up to 10 ft long

Przewalski's horse

This wild horse may be an ancestor of the domestic horses we all know, but has not been seen on the plains of Mongolia since 1968. It died out in the wild because of centuries of hunting and grazing of its pastures. Hundreds have been kept in zoos, however, where they have bred well. There are plans to return a few of them into their old Mongolian home.

FOUND IN:
Mongolia

SCIENTIFIC NAME:
Equus przewalskii

MAIN THREATS:
Hunting and habitat disruption

SIZE:
6–6½ ft long

Great bustard

The great bustard lives on open, grassy steppes. But as farming land increases it is gradually being pushed out. Weed killers, for example, are destroying much of its food and cover. Cattle often disturb it from its nest, and because it does not fly well (at up to 40 pounds it is the world's heaviest bird), it often collides with hazards like overhead cables.

FOUND IN:
Southern Europe to central Asia

MAIN THREATS:
Habitat destruction and disturbance

SCIENTIFIC NAME:
Otis tarda

SIZE:
2 ½–3 ¼ ft long

71

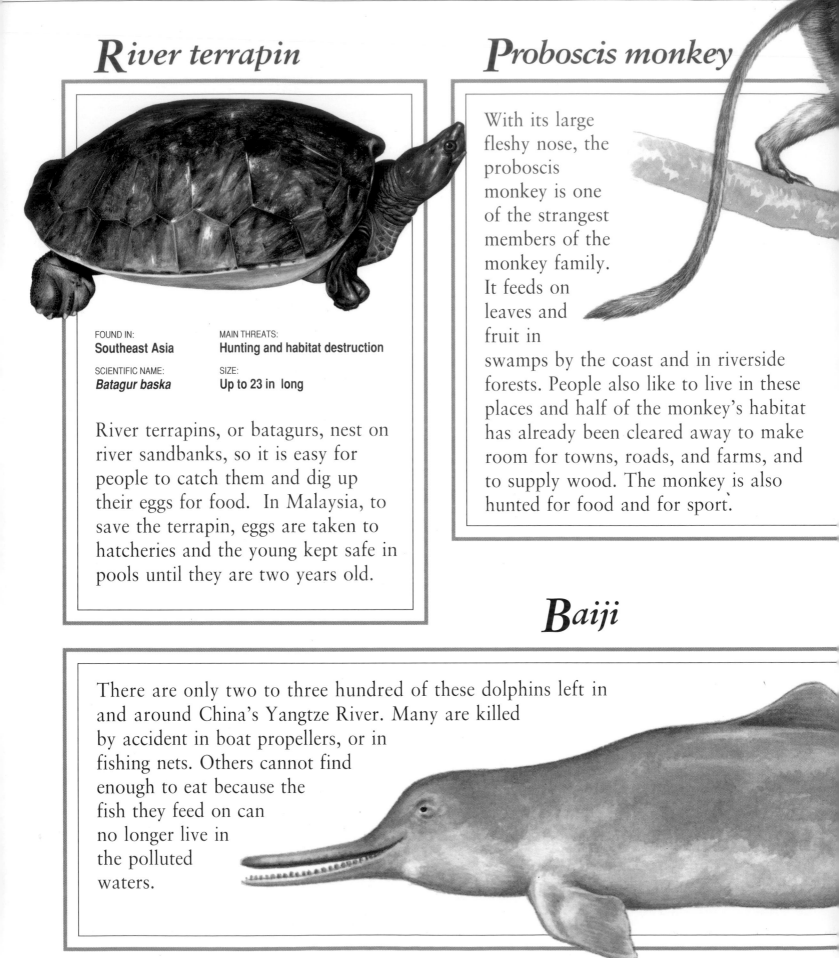

River terrapin

FOUND IN:
Southeast Asia

MAIN THREATS:
Hunting and habitat destruction

SCIENTIFIC NAME:
Batagur baska

SIZE:
Up to 23 in long

River terrapins, or batagurs, nest on river sandbanks, so it is easy for people to catch them and dig up their eggs for food. In Malaysia, to save the terrapin, eggs are taken to hatcheries and the young kept safe in pools until they are two years old.

Proboscis monkey

With its large fleshy nose, the proboscis monkey is one of the strangest members of the monkey family. It feeds on leaves and fruit in swamps by the coast and in riverside forests. People also like to live in these places and half of the monkey's habitat has already been cleared away to make room for towns, roads, and farms, and to supply wood. The monkey is also hunted for food and for sport.

Baiji

There are only two to three hundred of these dolphins left in and around China's Yangtze River. Many are killed by accident in boat propellers, or in fishing nets. Others cannot find enough to eat because the fish they feed on can no longer live in the polluted waters.

FOUND IN:
Borneo

MAIN THREAT:
**Habitat destruction
and hunting**

SCIENTIFIC NAME:
Nasalis larvatus

SIZE:
**Body 21–30 in long,
tail 22–30 in**

Mekong catfish

This catfish can grow to more than eight feet in length. But full-size fish are rare now in the Mekong River and its tributaries. Each year the adults swim upriver to spawn, and fishermen set traps to catch as many as possible when they return downstream. The fish are not only taken as food; the oil in their bodies is also valuable.

FOUND IN:	MAIN THREAT:	SCIENTIFIC NAME:	SIZE:
Southern China and Southeast Asia	**Overfishing**	*Pangasianodon gigas*	**Up to 8 ft long**

White-eyed river martin

FOUND IN:	MAIN THREATS:
Thailand	**Capture and habitat destruction**

SCIENTIFIC NAME:
Pseudochelidon sirintarae

SIZE:
**Body 6 in long,
tail 3 in**

FOUND IN:
China

SCIENTIFIC NAME:
Lipotes vexillifer

MAIN THREATS:
**Accidents and
habitat disruption**

SIZE:
6 ½– 8 ft long

This bird was unknown until 1968 when ten birds were discovered among the large flocks of swallows that roost in the reeds of Lake Boraphet. Since then, few have been found, and they must be close to extinction. There are also fewer swallows on the lake because people trap them and harvest the reeds. These problems probably affect the martins as well.

Australia and New Zealand

The settlers who sailed to New Zealand and Australia brought many problems for the animals that lived there.

Since the late eighteenth century, all sorts of problems have plagued the wildlife of Australia and New Zealand. For hundreds of years, local peoples had left much of the landscape unchanged. But then European settlers began to colonize the land. They laid out farms and ranches where there had once been grasslands and forests. They shot large numbers of wild animals for food and sport, and to protect their livestock.

The biggest threats to native wildlife, however, were the animals and plants that the newcomers brought with them. Sheep and goats grazed pastures so short that they drove out many grass-eating and seed-eating animals. Rats, weasels, cats, and foxes found native animals easy to catch. These and other introduced predators have put ten of the seventeen species of birds that live on New Zealand's Chatham Islands in danger of extinction. Foreign grasses have replaced most of New Zealand's natural tussock grass and the rubber vine has infested Australia's rain forests, making the habitat less suitable for native species.

In 1879, the Royal National Park was established near Sydney. Since then, great efforts have been made to protect wildlife. Conservationists are working hard in both countries to preserve habitats and rebuild the populations of vulnerable species.

Leadbetter's possum lives in hollows in old eucalyptus trees. But if its forest home continues to be destroyed as trees are felled for timber, this already rare animal is in danger of disappearing completely.

Problems in Australia and New Zealand

There is a common threat to the survival of the various endangered animals of Australia and New Zealand. Too often, animals brought from overseas and let loose to roam the land have played a part in the downfall of native creatures. The greater bilby, which was once common in Australia, suffered terribly because of hunting and cattle grazing. But then more problems came from introduced animals. Rabbits took over bilby burrows, foxes attacked it, and the bilby is now extinct in many areas. In others it lives only in scattered pockets.

The ring-tailed rock wallaby feeds on the scant plant life in dry, rocky country. It first came under threat from hunters who wanted its handsome fur. Now its main enemies are goats that have invaded its habitat, using up its food supply.

Smaller mammals have also suffered. The numbat has retreated to the southwest corner of Australia. There it uses its strong claws to break into termites' and ants' nests and its long snout to probe inside and eat the occupants. Foxes and cats, as well as fires set to clear land, made life impossible for the numbat in other regions.

Birds are also at risk. The malleefowl is famous for building mounds of rotting vegetation where it keeps its eggs warm. Much of its scrubland

(1) Malleefowl

(4)

(3)

(2)

(1)

(7)

(7) Numbat

(6) Hochstetter's frog

76

(2) Greater bilby

(3) Ring-tailed rock wallaby

home has been turned into cropland or is heavily grazed by sheep and rabbits.

Hochstetter's frog lives along forested mountain streams in New Zealand's North Island. It has been wiped out in many areas by rats, and pigs and goats have ruined much of the streamside vegetation. Clearing of New Zealand's forest for farming left little room for the kokako. Only about one thousand birds remain on North Island. The southern group was thought to be extinct until some were discovered recently on Stewart Island. All the survivors, however, risk attack from rats and cats that raid nests.

Efforts are under way to help most of these animals. One that has already benefited is the estuarine crocodile. This giant animal is heavily hunted for its hide along the coast of Asia, but because of a strict hunting ban far fewer are killed in northern Australia. It is one of the few places in the world where crocodiles are actually rising in number.

(6)

(5)

(4) Estuarine crocodile

(5) Kokako

Tuatara

Although it looks like a lizard, the tuatara belongs to a much older group of reptiles, known as the "beaked reptiles." All except the tuatara died out long ago, and when settlers brought new animals to New Zealand the tuatara nearly disappeared as well. Rats, especially, ate so many eggs and young that the tuatara was wiped out on the mainland. Today it survives on about 30 small islands, where constant efforts are made to keep rats out.

FOUND IN:
New Zealand

MAIN THREATS:
Introduced animals

SCIENTIFIC NAME:
Sphenodon punctatus

SIZE:
Up to 26 in long

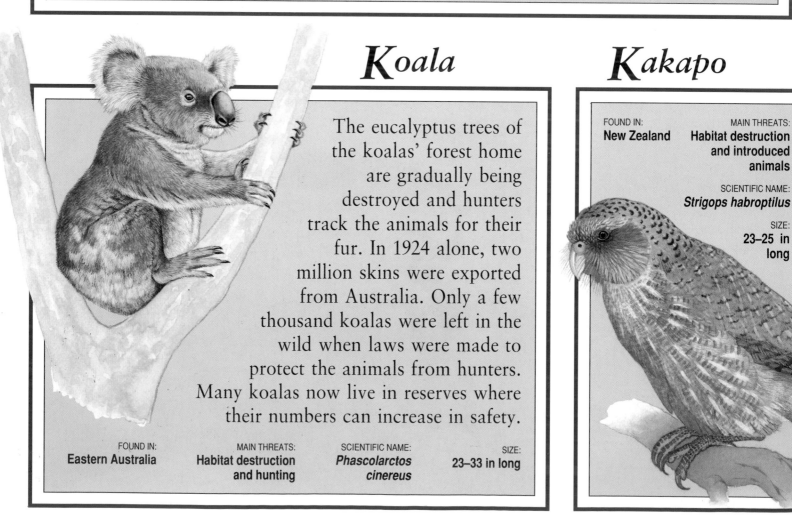

Koala

The eucalyptus trees of the koalas' forest home are gradually being destroyed and hunters track the animals for their fur. In 1924 alone, two million skins were exported from Australia. Only a few thousand koalas were left in the wild when laws were made to protect the animals from hunters. Many koalas now live in reserves where their numbers can increase in safety.

FOUND IN:
Eastern Australia

MAIN THREATS:
Habitat destruction and hunting

SCIENTIFIC NAME:
Phascolarctos cinereus

SIZE:
23–33 in long

Kakapo

FOUND IN:
New Zealand

MAIN THREATS:
Habitat destruction and introduced animals

SCIENTIFIC NAME:
Strigops habroptilus

SIZE:
23–25 in long

Lumholtz's tree kangaroo

FOUND IN:
Northeastern
Australia

MAIN THREATS:
Habitat destruction

SCIENTIFIC NAME:
Dendrolagus lumholtzi

SIZE:
Body 20–24 in long,
tail 28 in

Unlike other kangaroos, the tree kangaroo is happy to live high in the forest trees where it eats leaves and fruit. It can even sleep up there, crouched on a thick branch. This species has seen its rain forest home gradually shrink in area, mainly because of logging. But there are now several forest parks and reserves where it should be safe.

Ghost bat

FOUND IN:
Northern Australia

MAIN THREATS:
Habitat destruction
and disturbance

SCIENTIFIC NAME:
Macroderma gigas

SIZE:
4–5 ½ in long

This parrot no longer lives on mainland New Zealand, partly because much of its forest home has been destroyed. And because it lives on the ground and cannot fly, it is easy prey for introduced dogs, cats, rats, and ferrets. The 43 birds that are left have been taken to two islands for safety. It is hoped that they will breed there, but attempts so far have not been successful.

The ghost bat gets its name because of the strange color of its pale fur at night. It flies over all kinds of terrain from forest to desert. By day, the bat roosts inside caves, rocky clefts, and old mine shafts, but it is easily disturbed by people. Quarrying (removing stone) has destroyed some of its most important roosts. Of the several thousand bats that survive, 1,500 live in an abandoned gold mine that may soon be re-opened.

79

Focus on: *Dugong*

The waters off northern Australia are the last place of refuge for the dugong. This placid sea mammal used to be seen in warm coastal waters all around the Indian and western Pacific oceans. But its numbers have dwindled everywhere, and along many stretches of coast it is in danger of extinction. Though there are several thousand dugongs around Australia that sometimes appear near the shore in large herds, even this population seems to be getting smaller.

Slow-moving, vulnerable and with a low breeding rate, the dugong simply has trouble surviving in a world ruled by humans. People obstruct the shallows with nets, pollute and damage the sea grasses on which it feeds, and hunt the animal for meat. Only aboriginal peoples are allowed to hunt the dugong in Australia, but some conservationists think that even they kill too many. The best way to save the dugong is probably to create special marine reserves where its habitat is undisturbed, and hunting and net fishing are banned.

Browsing in the shallows
The dugong eats little but the leaves and roots of sea grass, which grows in beds in shallow coastal waters. Unfortunately, areas of sea grass are being increasingly ruined by pollution, dredging, and burial under sediments.

Innocent victim
Lethal nets designed to keep sharks away from Australian bathing beaches are just one of the many dangers that threaten the dugong. Since 1975 about one dugong a month has been killed by becoming entangled in a net and drowning. On some parts of the coast the dugong is now extremely rare.

Broad-headed snake

This colorful snake's poison is very strong. It lives near the city of Sydney, and people sometimes kill it out of fear. But the biggest threat is that people take the rocks under which it shelters by day to decorate their gardens. In some places it no longer has anywhere to hide.

FOUND IN:	MAIN THREATS:	SCIENTIFIC NAME:	SIZE:
Southeastern Australia	Habitat disruption	*Hoplocephalus bungaroides*	Up to 24 in long

Stick-nest rat

This rat has disappeared from the mainland. Many of the places it lived have been made into farmland. Cattle trampled its nests, farm animals and rabbits chewed the juicy plants it eats, and it was attacked by cats and foxes. The rat survives only on Franklin Island, and if its enemies reach the island, it will probably become extinct.

FOUND IN:
Southern Australia

MAIN THREATS:
Habitat destruction and introduced animals

SCIENTIFIC NAME:
Leporillus conditor

SIZE:
Body 7–10 in long, tail 6–7 in

Gouldian finch

FOUND IN:
Northern Australia

MAIN THREATS:
Capture and disease

SCIENTIFIC NAME:
Chloebia gouldiae

SIZE:
5 in long

Flocks of this beautiful finch busily forage for grass seeds in the hottest weather. Sadly, fewer and fewer birds now live in the wild. This may be because many were trapped for sale as cage birds and often died on the way to the pet shops. But scientists have now found that many of these finches are infested with a dangerous parasite. This disease may have spread to the wild flocks from escaped cage birds.

Takahe

FOUND IN:
New Zealand

MAIN THREATS:
Introduced animals

SCIENTIFIC NAME:
Porphyrio mantelli

SIZE:
23–25 in long

New Zealanders thought the flightless, seed-eating takahe was extinct, but in 1948 some birds were rediscovered on South Island. With careful conservation, their numbers have risen there to about 260, and some birds that were raised in captivity have been set free. It is important to keep the takahes' two main enemies at bay—stoats, which attack them, and red deer, which eat their food.

Bridled nail-tail wallaby

This wallaby has a strange way of hopping, moving its arms in circles as it bounces. It used to be widespread, but it died out in areas where heavy grazing by sheep and cattle affected its grassy shrubland habitat. Now it roams across just 27,000 acres of land in central Queensland. Even some of this may be cleared for cattle pasture.

FOUND IN:
Northeastern Australia

MAIN THREATS:
Habitat destruction

SCIENTIFIC NAME:
Onychogalea fraenata

SIZE:
Body 17–27 in long, tail 13–26 in

83

Oceanic Islands

Islands can be dangerous places for wildlife, but their small size may make them ideal conservation areas.

The small, remote islands that lie far out in the oceans are home to many endangered animals. Because space is in short supply, these animals exist in very small populations, and most do not live anywhere else. This puts each species at risk. A volcanic eruption or a fierce storm could wipe out the entire population overnight.

Usually, however, the changes caused by people are the greatest threat. As the human population of the islands grows, more and more natural habitats disappear. The goats, pigs, sheep, and cattle that people keep eat away native vegetation. Few island plants have stinging hairs, prickles, or a bitter taste to deter large plant eaters.

Other introduced animals kill wildlife directly. Most native island creatures are not used to such enemies as rats, cats, and mongooses, and they have few defenses. Many of the birds, for example, cannot even fly. Some do not recognize danger. The now extinct dodo, which lived on the island of Mauritius in the Indian Ocean, was so unafraid that sailors could walk up and club it to death for food.

Conservation on oceanic islands has been slow to start, but there are already hopeful signs. Strict protection in the Galapagos Islands is helping many unique species. And Cousin Island in the Seychelles was set aside for conservation in 1968. Since then the island's population of the rare Seychelles brush warbler has already greatly increased.

Pollution and attacks from dogs and cats could greatly harm the marine iguana, which lives on rocky shores in the Galapagos Islands. Conservationists work hard to keep threats like these at bay.

Problems in Oceanic Islands

As in Australia and New Zealand, the dramatic decline of native wildlife in oceanic islands is partly due to the introduction of new animals. These animals often hunt native species or intrude on their habitat.

The story of Hawaii shows us how vulnerable island wildlife can be. Many Hawaiian animals began to decline more than a thousand years ago when Polynesian settlers started to hunt and farm on the islands and let rats loose there. By the time Europeans arrived, one half of its bird species had been driven to extinction. Several more have since followed. The akiapolaau is one of the survivors, but only just. It now lives only in small patches of old forest invaded by goats, sheep, and pigs.

On other, smaller islands nature is just as fragile. On Christmas Island, mining has destroyed a large part of the forest where the Abbot's booby nests. Its population has fallen to just fifteen hundred pairs. The tiny inch-long Seychelles frog has lost most of its mountain forest home to farming and is also harmed by introduced animals including exotic frogs that take over its habitat.

Cats wiped out the Ascension frigatebird on Ascension Island. Now this seabird nests only on Boatswainbird Island, a rocky islet just off shore. If cats arrived there it would quickly die out. The same thing could happen to the Inaccessible Island rail if cats or rats ever reached its remote island home.

Sea creatures are usually less vulnerable because they are more widespread and

① Seychelles frog

⑦ Galapagos giant tortoise

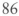

⑥ Inaccessible Island rail

(2) Abbott's booby

numerous, but not all are safe. The giant clam, which can weigh more than 440 pounds, has disappeared from some coasts because people have taken so many for their meat and their shells.

Efforts are under way to conserve the Galapagos giant tortoise. It has suffered from hunting, habitat destruction, and egg-stealing predators, but is being helped by strict protection from introduced animals and by captive breeding.

(3) Giant clam

(4) Ascension frigatebird

(5) Akiapolaau

87

*F*ijian banded iguana

This long-tailed lizard is a good tree climber, with long toes to give it a firm grip. But iguanas can no longer hide from their enemies because trees on its islands are being burned and felled, and goats browse heavily on the remaining plants. Its worst enemy is the mongoose, which eats both eggs and young. Wherever the mongoose has been released, the iguana is very rare.

FOUND IN:
Fiji and Tonga (Pacific Ocean)

MAIN THREATS:
Introduced animals and habitat destruction

SCIENTIFIC NAME:
Brachylophus fasciatus

SIZE:
Up to 35 in long

*K*auai o-o

FOUND IN:
**Hawaii
(Pacific Ocean)**

MAIN THREATS:
**Habitat destruction and
introduced animals**

SCIENTIFIC NAME:
Moho braccatus

SIZE:
7–8 in long

One hundred years ago, this darting, insect-eating bird was common all over Kauai island in Hawaii. But much of its rain forest home was destroyed and black rats invaded the island. The rats raided nests and killed adults, nearly causing the o-o to become extinct. A small group of birds was discovered in 1960, but it was too late to save the o-o. In 1989, only one solitary male could be found.

Tooth-billed pigeon

This pigeon spends most of its time on the ground, where it eats leaves, seeds, and berries. It has a hooked bill similar to that of the dodo and, like that extinct island bird, the tooth-billed pigeon has been hunted for its meat. It has also suffered from the release of harmful animals such as cats and rats that attack the bird, and pigs that ruin its nests.

FOUND IN:	MAIN THREATS:	SCIENTIFIC NAME:	SIZE:
Western Samoa (Pacific Ocean)	**Hunting and introduced animals**	**Didunculus strigirostris**	**13 in long**

Mauritius kestrel

FOUND IN:
Mauritius (Indian Ocean)

MAIN THREATS:
Habitat destruction

SCIENTIFIC NAME:
Falco punctatus

SIZE:
11–13 in long

The Mauritius kestrel, which hunts in dense forest for lizards and small birds, has been at brink of extinction. In 1986, there were just six wild kestrels left on the island in untouched forest on mountain slopes. But many more were being raised in cages and have since been set free. Now the wild population stands at nearly 200.

Rodrigues flying fox

In 1974, when there were fewer than 80 alive, the Rodrigues flying fox was probably the rarest bat in the world. It eats fruit and needs plenty of trees so it can find food all year round, but only a tiny part of Rodrigues Island is still forested. The bats' roosting site is now protected and new fruit trees have been planted to provide it with food. Numbers of this bat are now believed to have risen to about 400.

FOUND IN:	MAIN THREATS:
Rodrigues Island (Indian Ocean)	**Habitat destruction**
SCIENTIFIC NAME:	SIZE:
Pteropus rodricensis	**6 ½–8 in long**

Focus on: *Hawaiian goose*

At the end of the eighteenth century, there may have been 25,000 Hawaiian geese. But settlers came to Hawaii and turned the land into farms and ranches. They introduced grazing animals and predators, and they hunted the goose for meat. The birds seemed to be doomed. One of their worst enemies was the mongoose, which was released on the islands to kill rats on sugar plantations but soon started killing the native animals. By 1947, only about thirty wild geese remained.

But all was not lost. Special captive-breeding projects for the geese were started at Pohakuloa in Hawaii and at Slimbridge in England. Eventually there were enough captive birds to start releasing them into the wild. Today there are up to five hundred geese flying free on the high, open slopes of the islands of Hawaii, Kauai, and Maui. However, the future of the Hawaiian goose, also known as the nene, is still at risk.

Conservationists have tried to keep introduced animals away (sometimes by trapping them), but the geese that have been released still have not been able to raise many young.

Help at hand
Numbers of the Hawaiian goose have increased thanks to an international rescue effort. At the Slimbridge breeding center in England (above) as well as in Hawaii, hundreds of geese have been reared since the 1950s. Many have been released back into the wild. In their native Hawaii busy roads can be another danger (left).

Deadly intruder
Nesting Hawaiian geese have little defense against an attacking mongoose. This swift-moving hunter can easily steal eggs and chicks and can even kill an adult goose if it is molting and unable to fly.

St. Helena earwig

FOUND IN:
St. Helena (Atlantic Ocean)

MAIN THREATS:
Unknown

SCIENTIFIC NAME:
Labidura herculeana

SIZE:
2–3 in long

In 1798 a giant three-inch earwig was spotted on the remote island of St. Helena, but it was not until 1965 that the insect was found again. Little is known about the insect but it seems to live only in a tiny, barren area in the northeast of the island. The earwig has long forceps on its head but no wings. It lives in burrows, and comes out at night—but only in the rainy season.

Hawaiian hawk

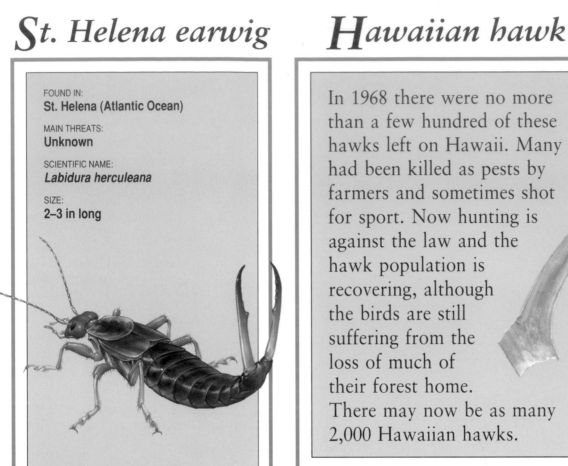

In 1968 there were no more than a few hundred of these hawks left on Hawaii. Many had been killed as pests by farmers and sometimes shot for sport. Now hunting is against the law and the hawk population is recovering, although the birds are still suffering from the loss of much of their forest home. There may now be as many 2,000 Hawaiian hawks.

FOUND IN:
Hawaii (Pacific Ocean)

MAIN THREATS:
Habitat destruction

SCIENTIFIC NAME:
Buteo solitarius

SIZE:
16–18 in long

Land iguana

The land iguana chews plants, including spiny cacti, and has a strong body for digging burrows in the earth. In the past, it was hunted for sport and for its

Flightless cormorant

FOUND IN:
Galapagos (Pacific Ocean)

MAIN THREATS:
Accidents and introduced animals

SCIENTIFIC NAME:
Nannopterum harrisi

SIZE:
34–35 in long

With its small, ragged wings this cormorant is not able to fly, but up until now it has not needed to. It lives on rocky coasts and simply dives into the water to catch octopus and other seafood when it is hungry. But the cormorants might not be safe in the future. Local fishermen may soon be allowed to use nets, which could easily entangle the birds, and introduced dogs could damage the nesting colonies.

flesh (especially its tail). This, along with attacks on its young by dogs, cats, and rats, led to its disappearance from many Galapagos islands. On the islands where it survives, goats are its main enemy—they eat the plant life, leaving little for the iguana.

FOUND IN:
Galapagos (Pacific Ocean)

MAIN THREATS:
Hunting and introduced animals

SCIENTIFIC NAME:
Conolophus subcristatus

SIZE:
Up to 3 ½ ft long

Robber crab

This big land crab lives under rocks or in burrows on tropical islands. Islanders love to eat the crab and it has been hunted so heavily that it has disappeared completely from

Mauritius. Now some of the other islands have laws to protect the robber crab from hunters.

FOUND IN:
Indian Ocean and Pacific Ocean islands

MAIN THREATS:
Hunting

SIZE:
Up to 3 ft legspan

SCIENTIFIC NAME:
Birgus latro

Resource List

A bibliography is not included in this book since information about endangered species is constantly changing. *The World Wildlife Fund Guide to Endangered Species* is one good source for more information; recent periodicals are the most current. Environmental and conservation organizations, some of which are listed below, are also useful sources. These organizations have limited funds and materials, and most prefer written requests for information. When writing, please include self-addressed stamped envelopes, and be patient while waiting for a response. *The Conservation Directory*, published by the National Wildlife Federation, lists more organizations.

✍ Answers children's inquiries   ✉ Periodicals for children   ♥ Special membership for children

ORGANIZATIONS FOR THE CONSERVATION OF A PARTICULAR SPECIES

American Cetacean Society ✍
P.O. Box 2639, San Pedro, CA 90731 (310-548-6279)
Protects marine mammals, especially whales, dolphins, and porpoises. Will send information requested by individuals and classrooms.

Bat Conservation International ✍
500 Capital of Texas Highway North, Building 1, Suite 200, Austin, TX 78746 (512-327-9721)
Elementary educator's package includes a video and book. Other materials also available. Please write for catalog.

Ducks Unlimited, Inc. ✍ ✉ ♥
One Waterfowl Way, Memphis, TN 38120 (901-758-3825)
Conservation of waterfowl and wetlands. Children's membership includes *Puddler* or *Ducks Unlimited* magazine. Gives information about local conservation events for children.

Friends of the Sea Otter ✍
P.O. Box 221220, Carmel, CA 93922 (408-625-3290)
Offers information packets for different ages.

International Crane Foundation ✍ ♥
E-11376, Shady Lane Road, Baraboo, WI 53913, (608-356-9462)
Will send fact sheets about different species of cranes. Seven curriculum packets and various audio/visual educational materials available. Individuals and classrooms may participate in an "Adopt-a-Crane" program.

Raptor Education Foundation, Inc. ✍
21901 East Hampden Avenue, Aurora, CO 80013 (303-680-8500)
Uses birds of prey, such as hawks and falcons, in educational lecture programs that travel nationwide to emphasize the importance of raptors. Regularly visits schools with this presentation. Offers a coloring album.

Save the Dolphins Project ✍ ♥
Earth Island Institute, 300 Broadway, Suite 28 San Francisco, CA 94133 (415-788-3666)
Trying to end death and injury of dolphins due to international tuna industry. Coordinated national canned tuna boycott. Also has a sea turtle restoration project.

Wild Canid Survival and Research Center/ Wolf Sanctuary
P.O. Box 760, Eureka, MO 63025 (314-938-5900)
Breeds and maintains endangered wolves for possible use in reestablishment efforts. Also serves as research and educational facility. Gives presentations and tours of sanctuary to schools and groups. Offers a children's packet and various educational packets for junior high age and older.

GENERAL CONSERVATION ORGANIZATIONS

African Wildlife Foundation ✍
1717 Massachusetts Avenue, N.W., Suite 602 Washington, DC 20036 (202-265-8393)
Operates wildlife projects in Africa, assists national parks, and conducts conservation education programs in schools. Fact sheets are available.

Center for Marine Conservation, Inc. ✍
1725 DeSales Street, N.W., Suite 500 Washington, DC 20036 (202-429-5609)
Protects whales, dolphins, seals, sea turtles, sea birds. Newsletters, fact sheets, and many types of educational materials for classrooms and young people available.

The Cousteau Society, Inc. ✉ ♥
870 Greenbriar Circle, Suite 402, Chesapeake, VA 23320 (804-523-9335)
Produces television films, does research, gives lectures, and publishes books and other materials. *Dolphin Log* magazine for children with membership.

Defenders of Wildlife ✍
1244 19th Street, N.W., Washington, DC 20036 (202-659-9510)
Protects endangered species such as wolves, desert tortoises, and Florida panthers. Protects marine life from plastic pollution and drift nets. Offers information for children, including fact sheets about endangered species.

Environmental Defense Fund, Inc. ✍
Attn: Public Information, 257 Park Avenue South New York, NY 10010 (212-505-2100)
Offers teacher's packets for grades K-6 and 7-12.

Greenpeace USA, Inc. ✉
1436 U Street, N.W., Washington, DC 20009 (202-462-1177)
Subscriptions available to *Peace Three* newsletter for ages 6-13.

National Audubon Society ✍
700 Broadway, New York, NY 10003
Activist-oriented. Various materials available for young people.

National Geographic Society ✉
17th and M Streets, N.W., Washington, DC 20036 (202-775-6701)
National Geographic World magazine for ages 8-14. Classroom materials, including learning kits, books, atlases, maps, filmstrips, videos, films, and computer software. Please write for catalogs.

National Wildlife Federation ✉
Attn: Ranger Rick Correspondence Division 8925 Leesburg Pike, Vienna, VA 22184 (703-790-4000)
Numerous periodicals, including two for children: *Your Big Backyard* (for very young readers) and

Ranger Rick. Children can write for more information, or with questions about animals/environment to *Ranger Rick.* Educational materials available.

Rainforest Action Network ✍
Attn: Information Department, 450 Sansome, Suite 700, San Francisco, CA 94111 (415-398-4404)
Works internationally with other environmental organizations to protect rain forests and the human rights of those living in them. Publications, teacher's materials, Children's Action Guide, fact sheets, and a catalog of gift items are available.

Smithsonian Institution ✍
1000 Jefferson Drive, S.W., Washington, DC 20560 (202-357-2700)
Operates a National Zoological Park in Washington, DC, which is developing programs to aid the survival of threatened and endangered species. Packet of information about tropical rain forests available.

Western Regional Environmental Education Council
c/o Don MacCarter, New Mexico Department of Game and Fish, State Capitol Bldg., Santa Fe, NM 87503 (505-827-7901)
Offers environmental education programs and materials for grades K-12. Please write for more information about Project WILD and Project Learning Tree.

The Wilderness Society ✍ ✉
900 17th Street, N.W., Washington DC 20056 (202-833-2300)
Nonprofit membership organization preserving wilderness and wildlife. *Greenfire* newsletter for older readers about endangered species. Fact sheets also available.

Wildlife Preservation Trust International, Inc. ✍ ✉ ♥
3400 West Girard Avenue, Philadelphia, PA 19104 (215-222-3636)
Preservation of endangered species through captive reproduction, research, education, fieldwork. Affiliated with the Jersey Wildlife Preservation Trust. Children receive the *Dodo Dispatch* magazine with membership as well as posters, pins, and a book about endangered species.

World Wildlife Fund, U.S.
1250 24th Street, N.W., Washington, DC 20037 (202-293-4800)
Will send children fact sheets about animals. Offers newsletters, atlases, books, and various audio/visual materials. Educational materials such as the "Vanishing Rain forests Education Kit" for grades 2-6 (includes a video) are available. Please write for catalog.

Index

Index

Acknowledgments

ILLUSTRATION CREDITS

Animal illustrations by:
Graham Allen, Alan Male, Colin Newman, Michael Woods

and Norman Arlott, Dianne Breeze, Malcolm Ellis, Robert Gilmor, Vana Haggerty, Peter Hayman,
Steve Kirk, Norman Lacey, Denys Ovenden, Myke Taylor, Dick Twinney, Owen Williams, Ken Wood

Maps:
Peter Ferris

Focus spreads:
Priscilla Barret: 46–47, 58–59, 68–69, 80–81, 90–91
Tudor Humphries: 22–23, 34–35

PHOTOGRAPHIC CREDITS

10 P. Morris/Ardea; 12 S. Morgan/Greenpeace; 13 Mark N. Boulton/Bruce Coleman;
16–7 Jim Simmen/ ZEFA-Allstock; 22 & 23 Matt Bradley/Tom Stack & Associates; 28–9 E.A. Janes/NHPA;
34t Jany Sauvenet/ NHPA; 34b Martin Wright/Still Pictures; 40–1 K. and K. Ammann/Planet Earth Pictures;
46 Peter Johnson/ NHPA; 47 Rob Hadley/Impact Photos; 52–3 Dennis Green/Bruce Coleman;
59 Geoff du Feu/Planet Earth Pictures; 62–3 Mark N. Boulton/Bruce Coleman; 69t John Mason/Ardea;
69b Richard Matthews/Planet Earth Pictures; 74–5 Jean-Paul Ferrero/Ardea;
80 D. Parer & E. Parer-Cook/Auscape International; 84–5 François Gohier/Ardea;
90 The Wildfowl and Wetlands Trust, Slimbridge; 90–1 Philippa Stott/NHPA.

The Publishers would also like to thank Jeff Black of The Wildfowl and Wetlands Trust, Slimbridge, UK for
help and advice on the Hawaiian goose; Sara O'Grady for providing information on the dugong; and
Rachel Ferraro for her invaluable editorial assistance.